'Are you surprised to see me Matte

'Not rea. .' He shrugged, as if facing her again was the easiest thing in the world—as if he hadn't spent the best part of the night locked in sensual dreams with her. 'I heard at dinner last night from Sophie that you worked here…' That would account for dreaming of her, Matteo decided, and then he remembered why they could never be.

She preferred her work to him.

'Are your clientele richer here, Bella?'

'They are.' Bella smiled. 'I wonder if even *you* could afford me now.'

'Oh, but I'm sure that I could,' Matteo said. 'Given that I'm looking to buy this hotel. In a few months time I may well be your boss…'

'Never!' Bella spat.

'Why are you suddenly so cross?' Matteo asked, his voice a low husk, his face far too close to hers, so close that he could feel her soft rapid breaths on his cheek. 'From what I remember we parted on *very* friendly terms.'

Playboys of Sicily

Taming Italy's most notorious men!

You won't want to miss this sizzlingly dramatic
new duet from *USA TODAY* bestselling author
Carol Marinelli—available only from
Mills & Boon® Modern™ Romance!

Tycoon Luka might agree to be ex-flame Sophie's
fake fiancé…but at what cost?

Sicilian's Shock Proposal
Available July 2015

Bella hasn't seen millionaire Matteo since *that* night.
He's as irresistible as ever, but will he still want her
after he discovers her secret?

His Sicilian Cinderella
Available August 2015

HIS SICILIAN CINDERELLA

BY
CAROL MARINELLI

Harlequin (UK) Limited's policy is to use papers that are natural, renewable and recyclable products and made from wood grown in sustainable forests. The logging and manufacturing processes conform to the legal environmental regulations of the country of origin.

Printed and bound in Spain
by CPI, Barcelona

MILLS & BOON

Published in Great Britain 2015
by Mills & Boon, an imprint of Harlequin (UK) Limited,
Eton House, 18-24 Paradise Road, Richmond, Surrey, TW9 1SR

© 2015 Carol Marinelli

ISBN: 978-0-263-24897-5

Carol Marinelli is a Taurus, with Taurus rising, yet she still thinks she's a secret Gemini. Originally from England, she now lives in Australia and is a single mother of three. Apart from her children, writing romance and the friendships forged along the way are her passion. She chooses to believe in a happy-ever-after for all, and strives for that in her writing.

Books by Carol Marinelli

Mills & Boon® Modern™ Romance

The Playboy of Puerto Banus
Playing the Dutiful Wife
Heart of the Desert
Innocent Secretary...Accidentally Pregnant

Playboys of Sicily

Sicilian's Shock Proposal

The Chatsfield

Princess's Secret Baby

Alpha Heroes Meet Their Match

The Only Woman to Defy Him
More Precious than a Crown
Protecting the Desert Princess

Empire of the Sands

Banished to the Harem
Beholden to the Throne

The Secrets of Xanos

A Shameful Consequence
An Indecent Proposition

**Visit the author profile page at
millsandboon.co.uk for more titles**

PROLOGUE

'You'll come with me?' Matteo checked. 'You'll meet me and Luka at the airport this morning?'

He couldn't quite meet Bella's eyes—not just because there was a bruise on her cheek that his hand had made, more that last night had left him feeling more open and exposed than Matteo was used to.

And yet, for the most part, there was no sense of regret.

Bella looked up at the man who had had her heart since she was sixteen. On her first day as a chambermaid at Brezza Oceana she had started her shift feeling awkward in her uniform and missing her friends from school, but at least her closest friend Sophie had started working there that day too.

Bella and Sophie had walked along a corridor, only to see a few of Malvolio's men coming towards them, including Matteo Santini and his half-brother Dino.

The young women had stepped back to let the group pass but even as they'd done so Bella had braced herself for what was to come.

Sophie was out of bounds. She had been promised to Luka and they would get engaged soon. Even though he lived in England, Luka was Malvolio's son and so they didn't say anything to her.

The lewd comments were instead all aimed at Bella, because they knew she was Maria Gatti's daughter and were aware of her mother's occupation.

Bella was more than used to it.

'Hey!' Matteo said sharply, and for a moment Bella thought he was speaking to her but then he turned to the group, his brother included, and there was anger in his rich, deep voice. *'Déjala en paz.'*

He told them to leave her alone and when Dino argued Matteo said it even more firmly. In fact, when Dino persisted, Matteo shoved him against the wall and, still holding his brother there, he briefly turned to Bella.

'Via via...'

He had told her, not unkindly, to go away and leave them. It was the only time he had really spoken to her, but even before then he'd had a little bit of her heart—if her mother had money for Malvolio, it was Matteo she would ring to come and collect it, rather than Dino.

'At least Matteo only takes the money,' her mother would say.

Yes, little by little, over the years, Matteo had collected pieces of Bella's heart and now finally he had taken it all.

Last night Matteo had made her his lover and he had been her first.

Yes, the night had started out in the cruellest of circumstances, but they had been circumstances that had been forced upon them.

The coastal town in Sicily's wild, wild west was ruled by Malvolio.

The game was called fear and the people were his pawns.

He owned the hotel and most of the businesses and was a cruel landlord to most of the town. Despite the idyllic surroundings, there was crime and corruption at every turn and it was also a dangerous world if you did not play by Malvolio's rules.

Yet somehow, together, they had made last night beautiful and now, this morning, Matteo had asked her to leave Bordo Del Cielo with him.

'I'll do my best to be there,' Bella said.

'We only have this one chance,' Matteo warned. 'If you stay, then no one can ever know that I offered for you to join me. If they know that I...' Matteo hesitated, because with Bella he used words he was not used to hearing, let alone saying. 'If Malvolio gets so much as a hint that I care about you then you will be in serious trouble.'

'I've said that I will do my best.'

Bella watched as he knotted his tie. Matteo always dressed well, far better than the rest—his suits were made in Milan and his shoes were handmade. Last night she had found out the reason why Matteo always looked more expensive than the others.

Last night he had told her things that could possibly have them both killed.

He slipped on his jacket. His suit was dark grey, almost black, and his thick cotton shirt was relatively uncrumpled for he had carefully hung up most of his clothes last night during his slow, teasing strip.

'I love the fabric...' Bella ran her fingers over his

jacket then slipped her hand inside to feel the cool silk lining. She was a skilled seamstress and had an eye for design, not that she got to practise it here. 'I could make that,' Bella said.

'I have the best tailor come from Milan once a year,' Matteo said, and then he chose not to argue because her nimble fingers had moved from examining his jacket and were exploring the tiny pleats beneath his leather belt and his want for her had become unrelenting because he was rising again. 'You probably could.'

'Come back to bed,' Bella said.

'No. There is no time.'

She watched as he ran a hand through his jet hair and it fell into perfect shape. Soon those eyes would be behind expensive dark glasses. That was how she knew him best but in the last few hours Bella had seen the real beauty in those dark grey eyes as they had made love to her.

The suits, the clothes, the designer stubble were all an image that Matteo had created merely to survive.

This morning he was asking her to join him and his close friend Luka for a new kind of life in London.

Bella knew that Luka would have asked Sophie to come with him.

Sophie, though, had told Bella that she and Luka were over and that she was making her way to Rome tonight. She had begged Bella to join her but Bella had said no, that she could not leave her mother.

Maria, even if she was only thirty-four, was frail and sick, though she did her best not to let it show.

Matteo had said to Bella that if it was what it took

to get Bella to leave then she could bring her mother along.

He would take care of them both.

Bella sat in a rumpled bed, wearing nothing but a smile on a morning when other hearts were breaking.

'The plane leaves at nine...' Matteo said, and he sat down on the bed and picked up a long strand of Bella's hair and tucked it behind her ear. 'Please be there.' Now he looked into Bella's vivid green eyes. They were clear, they were bright and he knew, if she stayed here in Bordo Del Cielo, very soon they would be faded and vacant.

'If you don't get away this morning, Malvolio will have you working in the bar tonight and I shan't be there to...'

Save you.

He didn't say the words out loud but they hung unsaid in the air between them.

'If you stay,' Matteo continued, 'then as of tonight you'll be working and I'm telling you now, Bella—I don't want to date a working girl, I don't want there to have been anyone else.'

'Double standards, Matteo...' Bella pointed out, given how they had arrived at this point.

'No.' He shook his head. 'That is how I feel. Bella, I want to make a completely new start. I am done with this way of living. Tomorrow Malvolio wants me to start to avenge all the people who spoke against him during the trial...'

Bella shivered.

Malvolio, Luka and Sophie's father Paulo had been in prison for the past six months awaiting trial—a lot had been said against Malvolio. The people had believed that there was enough against him that he would surely be put away for life.

Instead, he was back and taking charge again.

'I have to get out because I don't want to do the things he has planned for me,' Matteo reiterated. 'Kill once and you'll always be a killer. It's not who I want to be. I want an honest life and I am going to make something of myself. I'll have enough trouble explaining my own past, I don't want yours bringing me down.'

Harsh words perhaps but for Matteo they were honest ones.

He was offering her an out and he still did not know if she would take it so he made it very clear this was her one chance to be with him.

'Once a whore and you'll always…'

'I get it,' Bella said.

'Good,' he continued. 'And, for the record, I don't have double standards—I've never paid for sex. Last night was never about money.' He said it even as he emptied his wallet for her. He took out every note that he had and this morning he had plenty. He laid the wad of cash beside her on the bed. 'I'm giving you money to get out, not for last night. If your mother refuses to come you can give her this cash to help tide her over.'

Bella could still scarcely believe what he was offering. She was eighteen but Matteo Santini had long been her dream. Now he sat on the bed where they had made love and offered her a new life.

Was it foolish to dream that her life really would be with him? That what they had found in this room could survive the outside world?

It felt far from foolish. Now, as the clock nudged six, life felt terribly simple and as he took her naked, warm body in his arms, the future looked deliciously clear.

'I'll take care of you,' Matteo said, and his kiss promised her that he would.

The wool of his suit, the sharp scent of his cologne both wrapped around her and she was lost to his mouth.

It was a slow, lingering kiss that confirmed how they were both feeling because, had time not been against them, Matteo would have shed his clothes and joined her in the bed that had provided their haven last night.

Instead, he drew her in closer to him. Her body was pliant, lazily relaxed and soft, and he smiled down when he stopped kissing her, though he didn't release her from his firm embrace. 'Don't you dare go to sleep when I'm gone.'

'I shan't.' Bella smiled. 'Don't go just yet. Surely there is a little more time.'

She was nervous of Matteo leaving. Worried that once he stepped outside the door he might change his mind.

'I have to,' he said.

'What will Luka say?' Bella asked. 'He will surely try and talk you out of bringing us along.'

'I shan't be telling Luka until you are right by my side, Bella. This is my choice, it has little to do with him. If he says no, screw him, we forget London and just go to Rome. I'm leaving here so that I don't have to answer to anyone…' He looked so deeply into her eyes then and his words, though slow and measured, were also urgent. 'If your mother says no, that she cannot leave, then at least you have given her a choice. You need to get out now.'

Bella's response was her kiss. She loved him unshaven against her skin and how, as they sealed their agreement with their mouths, he pressed her back onto the pillow. Bella's fingers knotted in his damp hair and she tried to match the stroke of his tongue, but it had shifted from tender to the delicious threat of possession.

He simply could not get enough of the night they had made beautiful.

He swallowed her sighs as his hand burrowed into the sheet and moved between her legs and then his mouth moved to her ear.

'I owe you one for this morning,' Matteo whispered, because this morning she had made magic on him with her mouth. He then got back to kissing her so deeply, so thoroughly that she could not now think of his pleasure as his fingers slid inside her.

She was hot and swollen from last night and his fingers were the reverse of a balm for instead of soothing they made her ache all over again. A delicious ache, though, for she knew, from last night, how it would end. She knew now that the pressure he was building within her would have her collapse into a void somehow lined in velvet any minute now.

He loved how she whimpered, how her hand moved to his as his fingers grew rougher, yet they did not move to halt him, Bella simply wanted to feel the skill beneath her own palm.

'I want you again,' Bella begged as he worked her slick sex while, with his free hand, he lifted one slender leg and pushed her thigh open so that she was more available to his hand.

'No time…' Matteo was struggling to catch his breath. His intention had been to leave Bella hungry enough to follow him and also he wanted the scent of her on his fingers.

He had never intended to be so close to coming himself.

None more so than when she removed her hand from his and found his straining shaft and reached for his zipper, but he paused her in his own way—he slipped another finger in and stretched her swollen intimate flesh and in doing so made sure that the imminent pleasure was simply all Bella's.

Her thighs came together, entrapping his hand but not halting it. Her neck arched and he chased her mouth as it lifted and, capturing her open lips, he suckled her tongue. He felt her tiny quivers down below and yet he stroked longer and harder till she tightened around him over and over. He nearly came to the sensation as he remembered taking her last night and the feel of those same beats of pleasure around him.

His fingers slipped out of her and he slipped a hand under her calf, straightening her leg so that it collapsed, loose limbed, to the bed and he watched her eyes slowly open and a lazy, sated smile spread over her lips.

She had him.

Even if he had just taken her, somehow with that smile she had him and for a second, just for a second, because mistrust came as second nature to him, Matteo wondered if he was being played.

He trusted no one.

He never had.

Even his friendship with Luka was a guarded one and so he warned her.

'Don't let me down, Bella.'

'I shan't.'

'So I'll see you soon?' Matteo checked, yet she hesitated for a moment before she gave him a small nod.

'Don't ruin this, Bella,' Matteo warned. 'No second chances. You leave with me this morning or you leave here for good…' He tapped his head and Bella knew that if she didn't follow him Matteo was telling her she would be dismissed from his mind.

Tough talk, Bella thought, but she knew him better.

Matteo might have been promoted to Malvolio's right-hand man but she knew for sure now that beneath that cool exterior beat a beautiful warm heart.

No matter what others thought of him.

They had made love all night yet he was harder and more wanting as he left the room than when he had entered.

Bella lay there as the door closed and how she would have loved to rest, to fall asleep in sheets that held the scent of them, to wake up slowly later and to recall in vivid detail the bliss of last night…

Soon she would do just that, Bella told herself.

The memories of last night, though, for now she must put away. Tuck them into the pages of her heart and turn the key.

She would take them out and examine them later.

There was no time for that now.

And so, instead, Bella showered quickly and pulled on the tarty black dress that she had worn last night.

It smelt of the cheap perfume that Matteo had loathed so.

The lacy stockings and suspenders she had also worn Bella stuffed in her bag.

And, knowing how things must appear, she did what would surely be expected of her—Bella emptied the bar fridge of the tiny bottles of liquor and took the nuts and treats. She picked up the money that Matteo had left on the bed and peeled off a couple of notes and put them in her bag, some she stuffed in her bra and the rest...

Bella pulled the rubber stoppers off her ridiculously high sandals and rolled the rest of the cash into two tight tubes and squeezed them into her heels, then she replaced the stoppers and strapped on her sandals.

She allowed herself one last glance around the room before she closed the door—oh, she had been terrified on entering it. Her cheek had been smarting from his slap, there had been angry tears falling from her eyes but now she stood smiling as she saw the chairs they had pushed back so they could dance together and make up for all the nights they had not had.

Her first night of work had been a pleasure rather than the hell she had anticipated.

Bella took the elevator down and her nostrils tightened as she walked into the bar. It was filled with the stale scent of last night's celebrations that had been held to mark Malvolio's release from prison and his not-guilty verdict.

'How was it?' Gina asked, referring to her night with Matteo, and Bella simply didn't know how to answer such a question so she said nothing. 'I hope he paid you well…' Gina said. 'Given that he kept you all night.'

'I thought this one was on Malvolio.' Bella shrugged and went to walk off but Gina halted her.

'Are you trying to say that Matteo didn't give you a tip?' Gina frowned, clearly disbelieving Bella, and she held out her hand.

'I thought that we would get to keep the tips.'

'Half is for Malvolio and the rest we divide amongst us.' Gina snapped her fingers and Bella opened her bag and handed over the money that she had earlier separated from the pile.

'And?' Gina said.

Bella took out a few of the tiny bottles of liquor that she had taken. 'There,' Bella said, and again went to walk off but was abruptly halted. Her long black hair was caught and yanked by Gina and Bella found herself face against the wall.

'Don't bullshit me,' Gina said, and her hands searched Bella's breasts, easily locating the wad of cash that she had stuffed into her bra.

She took out the cash and then let go of Bella's hair and Bella turned around.

'Don't ever try to get one up on me again, Gatti. I know tricks that you haven't even thought of yet.'

How Bella hated the world she had almost entered.

'Here,' Gina said, as if nothing had just happened, and she peeled off a paltry number of notes and handed them to Bella. 'I'll see you tonight.'

No, you won't, Bella thought, but she nodded.

She walked home when she wanted to run but she forced herself to walk as if she had plenty of time on her side.

Out of the Brezza Oceana hotel Bella took the path that ran alongside the beach. Some fishermen were bringing in the morning's catch and she drew some lewd comments and whistles from them.

She ignored them.

Further along Bella walked, past a small wooded area and a path that led to a small cove. Oh, she would have loved to have gone down to the water to visit it one last time—to take the tiny secret path that only the locals knew about and drink in the view she loved before she left Bordo Del Cielo for good.

But there was no time to linger and, anyway, Bella thought, there would be no Sophie there to chat with.

Her best friend had left last night and Malvolio was back and nothing now could ever be the same. Bella knew, if she really wanted to get away, she must not draw attention to herself.

No one must guess that she and her mother would be fleeing today.

So instead of heading down the secret path she turned and took the hilly street towards home. A group of tourists was standing on the corner, clearly the worse for last night, and their responses to Bella were pretty much the same as the locals had been.

She did not blush.

Never had Bella admired her mother more—Maria had always walked with her head held high and now, on this early morning, Bella did the same.

She carried on up the hill, her ankle giving way on the high heels several times, yet she gave a smug smile to herself when she thought of the money in them.

Yes, Gina might know a few tricks but Bella's mother had taught her daughter so many more.

She actually laughed as she walked up the garden path, recalling her mother coming home some mornings and emptying out her shoes!

Her mother's heart had just about broken last night as Bella had dressed for work. Now Bella pictured her face when she told her mother that Matteo had offered them both a way out of Bordo Del Cielo.

They *were* leaving today.

Her head was spinning with possibilities as she stepped into the house but then, in one second, it all changed.

Like stepping off a merry-go-round, everything slowed down and, stifling a scream, Bella took in the chaos. Their house was always neat but now the hall table was overturned and the vase of flowers from their garden lay strewn on the floor. And there, in the middle, lay Maria.

'Ma!'

Bella dropped to the floor and cradled her mother. Blood was pouring out of a head wound and for a terrible moment Bella thought this must be Malvolio's work. Briefly she wondered if somehow he had found out that she had made plans to leave…

'I fell…' Maria slurred.

'Were you drinking again?' Bella asked, because her mother had been so ill lately but she had promised that she had stopped all that.

'No.'

It took a moment to register that her mother was only able to move one arm and when Bella saw that one side of her face was weak it dawned on Bella that at just thirty-four years of age her beautiful mother had suffered a stroke.

'I'll call for the doctor,' Bella said.

As they waited, Bella ran and got a blanket from her mother's bedroom and made her as comfortable as she could.

The doctor arrived and then he called for an ambulance. It was five minutes after nine as the ambulance blasted its way through the town and then took the road that ran the opposite way from the airport.

Bella knew that she would never get there now.

She held her mother's hand as she held in her tears.

Her chance to escape had gone. She thought of Matteo at the airport, waiting for them to arrive.

He was.

Matteo stood with Luka, scanning the small airport, just waiting for the sliding doors to open and for Bella to appear.

'We should go through,' Luka said.

'Soon,' Matteo responded.

'They're boarding.'

'I just have to make a call…' Matteo had Maria's number because he would call her before he came to collect any money for Malvolio. He waited and there was a small beat of hope as it rung out.

They must be on their way, Matteo thought, but after another twenty minutes all hope had gone.

'Final call,' Luka said.

When he could wait no more Matteo boarded.

'Have you ever flown?' Luka asked, frowning because his friend had always been so worldly, so completely ahead of everyone's games, but it had just dawned on Luka he had never seem him out of Bordo Del Cielo and also he could feel Matteo's tension.

'Never,' Matteo answered, then sat silent beside his friend as the plane taxied down the runway and lifted into the sky.

Matteo wasn't nervous about flying, or leaving Bordo Del Cielo.

It was stay and become what, till now, he had avoided—a killer.

Or leave everything behind.

He chose the latter.

CHAPTER ONE

Five years later

BELLA GATTI.

Matteo did not want to hear her name, yet tonight it had peppered the conversation.

Neither did he want to remember a love that had made him a fool.

And so he sat through his closest friend and business partner's small engagement party, which was being held at Luka's luxurious Rome penthouse, avoiding, as best he could, any references to an extremely chequered past.

Matteo and his girlfriend of three months, which was a bit of a record for him, had flown in from London for the occasion. Knowing that Luka and Sophie's engagement was an extravagant farce, Matteo just wanted the night to be over and done.

Sophie Durante had turned up at Luka's London office just a few days ago and demanded that, on her father Paulo's release from prison, Luka uphold their long-abandoned engagement for the little time that her father had left.

Had Luka sought advice from Matteo they would not be sitting here now.

He had not and so they were.

Paulo kept speaking about Sicily, or rather the beautiful west and the people he had known there. Matteo, doing his level best not let his mind return there, had kept guiding the conversation back towards his true passion.

Work.

No, his passion wasn't Shandy, the woman who sat beside him, even though she would prefer that it was.

Honest work was his passion.

Matteo's reputation in the business world was his most prized possession. He had clawed his way back from less than nothing. He had made something of himself after a violent, criminal past and nothing and no one would ever reduce him or drag him back to the ways of old.

'So when do you go to Dubai?' Luka asked.

'Sunday,' Matteo answered. 'Unless you'll be needing the plane.'

Luka understood the slight taunt behind Matteo's words—Matteo was convinced that Sophie wanted more than an engagement ring on her finger.

He didn't believe Sophie's sob story for a moment.

Matteo didn't believe in anyone.

'Sunday?' Shandy checked. 'But I thought you said that you didn't have a firm date yet.'

'I only just found out.' Matteo's jaw gritted. Shandy had got it into her head that she would be joining him on this business trip. If they wanted to share a room then a ring on her finger might well be required and he could feel her squirm in expectation. No doubt she was thinking that this sudden trip to Rome might have a deeper meaning.

'Where are you staying?' Paulo asked.

'Fiscella,' Matteo answered, referring to the luxurious hotel he had booked into.

'It's very romantic,' Shandy said, but Matteo quickly crushed that.

'Luka and I are thinking of buying it,' he explained to Paulo. 'It is a nice old hotel but it needs a lot of refurbishment. I want to check out a few things for myself.'

'Doesn't Bella work there?' Paulo asked Sophie, and Matteo took a belt of his drink.

Bella.

The sound of her name had his throat tighten, so much so that he had to think, he actually had to tell himself to relax, in order to swallow the sickly *limoncello* down.

He loathed the taste, it reminded him too much of home and that was a place he had spent the last five years doing his level best to forget.

He did not want to think about his past and certainly Matteo did not want to hear what Bella Gatti was up to.

He'd already been told.

A couple of months after leaving, his half-brother Dino had told him that Bella was a regular at the bar.

He had told him a few other things that had had the bile rising in Matteo's chest and burning the back of his throat, but he had kept his voice impassive when he'd spoken with Dino.

If his half-brother got even a hint that Matteo cared

then Bella would be punished for his leaving, just for the pleasure of Matteo being told.

He swallowed down the liquor as Sophie answered Paulo's question.

'She does,' Sophie said, and despite his best intentions not to delve further Matteo found himself asking Sophie a question.

'Doing what?'

'She's a chambermaid.' Paulo answered for his daughter. 'Isn't she, Sophie?'

'Well, I guess it gives her access to a richer clientele.' Matteo's response was surly and, taking Shandy's hand, he led her to the floor to dance.

He didn't want to dance.

He just wanted to get away from the conversation.

Rome glittered beneath them. He could feel the pulse from the street below and the guarded Matteo suddenly wanted to escape the shackles and to shed his skin. He wanted to take a moped and explore the ancient, beautiful city. He wanted to ride high up and stare down at the ancient buildings and ruins, to drink cheap wine and be younger than his thirty years— only he wanted to do all of this with Bella.

Oh, he was dancing with the wrong woman tonight.

And every night since… He halted his thought process, for he never went back in his mind.

He just could not escape the truth today—for five years, long before Shandy, every night he had danced with the wrong woman and now, though his integrity at work was never in doubt, his reputation with women preceded him.

No, he could not escape the memories of them.

Matteo recalled Bella's deep, slightly husky voice

as she had told him about her favourite place in the
world—a jewel deep in Bordo Del Cielo that he had
never bothered to explore—the ancient baths that the
Moors had built. She had told him how she would take
herself off there at times and pretend that she had lived
long ago, how she imagined the carved-out stone filled
with spring waters and the sex and debauchery that
must have gone on there.

Bella had played with his mind then and somehow
she played with it even now.

'I love Sophie's dress…'

Matteo did not blink as Shandy pulled him out of
introspection. Instead, he frowned at the intrusion
as Shandy did what she did best—spent money in
her head.

'I want something similar,' she explained. 'I asked
Sophie who made it. Gatti. She's an emerging designer, apparently. I want to wear her before everyone
else is. Tomorrow I want to see her studio…'

Studio?

Matteo's teeth ground down.

More like a boudoir.

'Let's go.'

'It's too early,' Shandy protested. 'Anyway, I'm enjoying myself. You never said that it was Paulo Durante's daughter that Luka was getting engaged to. I
never thought we would be dining with such a high-
profile criminal tonight. It's exciting…' Shandy said,
and then dropped her voice. 'A turn-on.'

'Then you didn't live through it,' Matteo hissed,
and dropped his arms. 'We're leaving now.'

He chose not to tell Shandy that Paulo was no big
fish—the old man had been Malvolio's puppet.

Malvolio had been the leader and had seen to it that Paulo had taken the fall for him.

And the reason they were here tonight was that Malvolio was Luka's father.

Luka felt that he had a debt to pay and Sophie had called it in.

'Thanks for this,' Luka said, as he saw Matteo out. Shandy had gone to top up her make-up and the two men stood, uncomfortable with small talk.

Neither liked that their past was catching up with them.

They had made strong, good lives in London.

It felt strange to be back in Italy. Even Rome felt too close to Bordo Del Cielo tonight.

'Will you let me know when the wedding is?' Matteo's voice was thick with sarcasm.

'There will be no wedding,' Luka said. 'I just agreed to an engagement. You can surely see for yourself how sick he is. It's a matter of days till all this is done and I can get back on with my life.'

'Why are you going through with it?' Matteo said. 'You owe her nothing.'

'I owe Paulo this,' Luka corrected.

'You owe that old fool nothing,' Matteo insisted. Bile was churning and his venomous words were aimed at himself, because he had been but a day away from being Malvolio's second man. 'Sophie is just like Bella, both are up to no good. I'm telling you that she lies,' Matteo said. 'She's not doing well, like she told you she was. That dress is not designer...'

'Please.' Luka shrugged. 'I'm not like you, I don't care for fashion and labels. You always were a dark, mistrusting bastard.'

'A good-looking bastard, though,' Shandy said as she returned. Matteo pulled on his jacket and checked his reflection in the mirror, and Luka gave a dry laugh.

'Yes, Matteo, you look good,' Luka said, and it was his turn to be sarcastic now.

Matteo and Shandy headed out to the street.

'I like that you dress well,' Shandy said, but her words simply irked.

Yes, he always had dressed better than the rest. His suits were the most expensive, his hair superbly cut, his stubble pure designer.

Bella Gatti knew why, though, for he had confided in her.

Never again.

His driver was waiting and opening the door but Matteo stood there in the street rather than getting in.

'I think it might be good to walk...'

'To walk?' Shandy shuddered at the thought. 'In these heels?'

'No, I would like a walk alone,' Matteo said. 'It's been a long time since I've been back in Italy.'

'Well, it doesn't suit you,' Shandy said, because he had been at his brooding best since the plane had touched down. 'Matteo, come to bed...' Her mouth moved in to persuade him but he dodged his head back.

'I'll be in later.'

No apology, no excuses, he just walked off into the night.

And he did what he wanted.

Matteo bought a bottle of wine, and though the grapes were not from Bordo Del Cielo, they were from the west. He hired a moped and drove up, ever up, and then he parked it atop Capitoline Hill and stared down at the illuminated view and there, unlit, the lone horseman. But, though ancient and beautiful, it was the wrong view he gazed upon and, of course, there wasn't Bella by his side.

He let himself remember, not all of it, not even a lot—but something more intimate than the sex they had shared, he recalled the woman.

Black hair, green eyes and a smile that was so unexpected.

Sophie was all Sicilian fire, whereas Bella was the chameleon, the actress, the survivor who had once made his black heart smile.

Not now, Matteo thought, taking a drink from the bottle, but cheap wine didn't work either.

Nothing deadened the ache.

She was here in this town, he knew it now.

Was she sleeping?

Or did she lie awake tonight, knowing that he was near and burning for him as he did for her?

What did it matter? he thought, tossing the bottle into a bin and heading back to the hotel.

They could never be now.

'Where have you been?' Shandy asked sleepily, as he came into the bedroom of the luxurious suite, flicking on the sidelight as he crept in after three.

'Walking,' Matteo said. 'Go back to sleep.'

'I ordered champagne,' she said. 'I thought you had brought me here to…'

Yes, there was an air of expectation from Shandy. The sheikh Matteo was meeting with had told him he was looking forward to meeting his partner. The shareholders too were braying for the wild Matteo Santini to tame his ways.

And though he had told her from the start that nothing would ever become of them, Matteo had stuck at things with Shandy for longer than he did usually, though the final hurdle was proving too daunting.

Yes, Matteo knew it was time to grow up and settle down.

And he would, Matteo told himself as he undressed. Just not yet.

He looked at the hotel suite with more than vague interest, given that Hotel Fiscella was a potential purchase that he and Luka were considering making. And so he noticed not just that the room was immaculate but that the turn-down service had been discreet. The curtains were drawn and there were chocolates and a flower by the bed that had presumably been on his pillow and there was a pleasing scent in the air.

He glanced at the note by the bed that informed him that the weather tomorrow would be stormy and hot and that if there was anything further required not to hesitate to call the desk, and it was signed...

Bella.

It could not be her, Matteo mused. Yes, while he had found out that she was a chambermaid at this very hotel Bella was still a very common name.

Was it *her* scent that lingered?

Was it her hands that had smoothed back the sheets and plumped the pillows? Matteo thought as he climbed into bed.

'When?' Shandy asked as he lay there. 'Your friend just got engaged...'

Matteo said nothing.

'I want a commitment, Matteo,' she pushed.

Now he turned his head on the pillow and spoke to the face next to his.

'Then you're with the wrong man.'

Had she slapped him, had Shandy risen from the bed and got dressed and got out, he might have admired her.

But there she lay, clinging on with her gel nails to the image of them that the paparazzi had created and to the man she'd hoped he would one day be.

Matteo Santini, the bad boy made good.

No, he hadn't made good, not yet.

Tonight, he was right not to ask Shandy to marry him for had he known where Bella lived, had he had Bella's number then, Matteo knew he would have been paying a late-night visit to the whore he was hard for now.

He turned to flick off the bedside light and looked again at the signed card and he ached for Bella in a way he never had for anybody else.

Matteo fell asleep trying not to think about a woman from the past.

And then the dreams started.

On many occasions over the years Bella had attempted to frequent Matteo Santini's dreams.

His subconscious kept perpetual guard, though.

So controlled was Matteo that even in sleep he did his level best to chase all thoughts of her away.

But even guards had to sleep at times and so, on occasion, Bella slipped through the net and would dance all night through his mind.

Some of his dreams were high-end fantasy—masquerade balls where the two of them would make love, familiar and yet unknown to each other, while others consisted of seamy situations where he watched from a distance as Bella struggled while he was held back and unable to intervene. But then there were the dreams that consisted only of memories and those were the ones that Matteo preferred.

Tonight he slept through all three.

Perhaps it was because her name had been brought up in conversation at dinner.

Or was it the knowledge that she was working in Rome as a chambermaid in the same hotel where he slept tonight?

Whatever the reason the dreams had started, they were different tonight.

The circus had come to Bordo Del Cielo. It was a strange dream, a new one, for there had been no circus that ever visited there.

And this was no circus like others for it was not animals and clowns that performed in his dreams; instead there were different beasts—the people he had grown up amongst.

There was his younger half-brother Dino, who had revealed Matteo's plans to Malvolio the first time Matteo had tried to escape.

There was his cruel stepfather, who loathed his mother's attention anywhere other than on him or Dino.

Matteo looked around and there was Luka dressed in an orange prison suit that he didn't belong in. He saw Sophie being paraded around the ring and she was wearing only Luka's shirt, just as she had been on the night of Malvolio, Paulo and Luka's arrests.

Luka and Sophie had been in bed at the time Luka's

home had been raided and she had been hauled out in front of the townsfolk. It had been clear to all what had taken place between the young couple.

There was Talia, a woman Matteo had once helped, and she waved to him but he did not return it. No one must ever know the truth as to how he had saved her family so he ignored her.

He didn't care for any of them.

Nothing and no one moved him—there was no mean streak to Matteo, he'd long ago learnt to simply not care.

So why did he stand, his expression impassive, as his eyes scanned the crowd for her?

For Bella.

He looked up and there she was, walking on a tightrope as the town cheered her on. Her glossy, raven hair trailed down her bare back. The small silver costume did not fully cover her and he could see, as could the crowd, that her small pert breasts had been oiled and glittered and were on show.

She looked terrified yet she pushed out a smile as Malvolio, the ringmaster, urged her on.

And then, to the glee of everyone, she lifted her leg and stretched it out and exposed her nakedness there as Malvolio pushed her to perform, to somersault for the braying audience.

There was no net.

She had no choice.

He watched as Bella gracefully somersaulted and then, steadying herself, she turned and dodged the swing of the trapeze and the people on it, reaching down to swoop and claim her. It was to no avail, though, for there, high up, out of Matteo's reach, were others and she had no choice but to perform for them.

Then he saw Dino climbing a ladder.

'*Saltare!*' Matteo called, but his plea for Bella to jump was drowned out by the cheering crowd.

All night he dreamt in vivid detail, though his body barely moved in the bed.

Matteo was more than used to nightmares but these were of a very sexual kind.

'*Saltere*, Bella…' he urged, but still she did not hear him. Her hair was shiny with sweat, her tiny costume was torn and her feet were bleeding despite the chalk. She was exhausted, Matteo knew, and yet still Malvolio pushed her and still the crowd demanded more.

Now, at the birth of dawn, just before Matteo's alarm was due to go off, finally she heard him and looked down to where he held out his arms.

'*Ti prenderò quando cadi,*' Matteo shouted to her.

I will catch you when you fall.

There was just the briefest hesitation from Bella when she saw him there in the crowd, but then he ran to stand beneath her and she gave a smile of relief and recognition. Then she let herself go and fell into his waiting arms.

And catch her he did.

Her body was warm and familiar; finally she was back in his arms. Though breathless from exertion she had breath enough left for their kiss and as their mouths met they crashed through the filthy circus floor and landed, deep in kisses, on a bed that was soft and clean.

Now, just before morning invaded, he got to live his favourite dream—and it was one of pure memory.

Matteo lay there, recalling that night of no sleeping. Slow dancing around the hotel room as they'd recreated a night that had never taken place—the Natalia street party where, at sixteen, she had told him that she waited for him, while, unbeknown to her, Matteo had been running to escape Bordo Del Cielo and the hellish existence he had been forced further into.

Bella had been eighteen when their lips had first met, and despite the rough start it had been a night of romance and intense arousal, a night where he had given in to her pleas and had taken her innocence.

It had been a night like no other.

He did not want to think about the money that had changed hands in the morning, neither did he want to think of Bella when he had first seen her that night. She had been wearing thick make-up, her small bust jacked up, and she had been doused in cheap scent as she'd stood behind the bar, with men leering at her.

No, he preferred what had gone on behind closed doors.

Making slow tender love, drowning in deep kisses, and he recalled the sob as he had made her his lover. The bruise on her cheek that he had made, now forgiven, because that night she had understood why.

It had been him or Malvolio.

Hard, he lay there and gave in to a favourite memory—their night had been all but over and he had showered and gone to dress, but instead of doing so he had returned to the bed and he had lain beside her. Matteo had been deep in thought because he'd been considering asking Bella to join him when he made his escape.

And then he had felt her. First the softness of her

hair and the warmth of her cheek moving down his stomach, kissing him all the way down.

Matteo sank into the dream or the memory of her mouth as he felt the soft warm nuzzle of lips and then the wetness of tongue tentatively swirling around his engorged head.

Was there any better way to be woken? Matteo thought, letting out a low moan as she skilfully took him deeper into her mouth and he slid past her throat.

He started to thrust to the pleasant sensations and his hand moved down to her hair but then reality invaded. For if he was being woken then he must be asleep and there hadn't been a moment of sleeping with Bella.

And neither had Bella's lips been skilful; instead, they had been curious and nervous at first. They had been too light, too rough, too slow but, oh, so blissful.

He started to surface from his dream.

He attempted an ascent while his body told him to linger a moment, to just give in and enjoy, except the memory was gone and it was the wrong lips on his straining shaft and he wanted them off him.

He pulled at the hair to halt, aware that something was wrong, but as he did so a slew of something wet and cold doused the heat between his legs and there was a shout of shock and horror from Shandy as she knelt up and shook off the sheet. Her blonde hair was drenched and suddenly Matteo was wide awake and sitting bolt upright.

'Mi scusi...' A maid was sobbing for forgiveness, explaining that she had tripped over the ice bucket stand beside the bed, as Matteo flicked on the side light.

'*Imbeccile,*' Shandy shouted, as the maid picked up the now empty ice bucket that she had knocked over the copulating pair.

'Go easy, Shandy,' Matteo said, but there was no chance of that. Shandy *would* cry over spilt water.

'Jobless imbecile.' Shandy continued her rant in furious Italian and she also upgraded Matteo's relationship with her. 'Because I'm getting you fired. How dare you come in without knocking, how dare you interrupt my fiancé and I—?'

'It was an accident,' the maid was pleading as she tried to rectify the chaos—the tray she had brought in and its contents lay strewn not just over the floor but on a wall. Thick black coffee was seeping into the carpet, pastries and ham were sliding down the bedside table but the main chaos came from Shandy. She had jumped out of bed, was pulling on a robe and heading through to the lounge, screaming at the maid to have it cleaned up by the time she was back and warning her over and over that she was about to be fired.

Matteo stood, wrapped in a sheet, as Shandy picked up the phone in the lounge and demanded that the maid's head be served on a silver platter, then she flounced off to the shower, leaving Matteo to deal with the rest.

'*Mi scusi,*' the maid said again. She was kneeling on the floor, trying to sort out the things, but Matteo was far from impressed with her attempts to apologise. He didn't believe she was sorry for a moment, though his words were not sharp when he addressed her, more wearied.

'Get up, Bella.'

CHAPTER TWO

HER LONG BLACK hair was falling out of her ponytail and covering her face, but nothing could have stopped him from recognising her, and Matteo watched her hands still as he said her name.

She bit her nails, Matteo noticed.

He remembered that she hadn't.

That night, with him, her nails had been short but neat.

Every inch of her body held the potential for such vivid recall yet he fought it even now.

'I said, get up.' This time his voice was harsh but better that than dropping down to his knees and taking her back in his arms.

He waited for her to apologise again, to plead for forgiveness, but instead she looked up and beneath the sheet Matteo grew to her gaze as for the first time in many years their eyes met again—how he wished that the rare mossy green of her eyes that had enthralled him might leave him cold now.

Not a chance.

Mi scusi...

'Stop apologising, Bella. We both know that that was no accident...'

'But of course it was,' Bella insisted, still on her knees and looking up. 'I did knock. I thought I heard someone call out for me to enter. I got a fright when I saw the sheets move and I tripped…' She looked at the empty bottle of champagne that had fallen to the floor. 'I am so sorry to have upset your fiancée. Was the water very cold?'

'It did its trick,' Matteo said. He was starting to lose his patience and taking her forearm he hauled her up to stand. 'Get up, Bella.'

The dousing of water certainly wasn't doing its trick now, for her skin was warm beneath his fingers and the scent of her, even after all these years, was familiar. Only how could that be, for that night she had been doused in cheap perfume?

He had bathed that scent away, Matteo recalled, even as he fought not to remember.

Instead, he inhaled the starch from her maid's uniform.

It did not help.

Possibly, Matteo decided, Bella was the only woman who could wear pale green with a cream apron and still make it look sexy. Her legs were bare but even the flat lace-up shoes failed to detract from the beauty of her long limbs. Her body was just as slender as yesteryear, her eyes were still so big in her face and those lips that should not be smiling, given the chaos she had just created, still melted him.

There was, even with Shandy in the bathroom, a want and a need to kiss the smile from Bella's face…

'Are you surprised to see me, Matteo?'

'Not really.' He shrugged as if facing her again was the easiest thing in the world, as if he hadn't spent the best part of the night locked in sensual dreams with her. 'I heard at dinner last night from Sophie that you worked here...' That would account for dreaming of her, Matteo decided, and then he remembered why they could never be.

She preferred her work to him.

'Are your clientele richer here, Bella?'

'They are.' Bella smiled. 'I wonder if even you could afford me now.'

'Oh, but I'm sure that I could,' Matteo said. 'Given that I'm looking to buy this hotel. In a few months' time I may well be your boss...'

'Never,' Bella spat.

'Why are you suddenly so cross?' Matteo asked, his voice low and husky, his face far too close to hers, so close that he could feel her soft, rapid breaths on his cheek and it reminded him of her first orgasm. 'From what I remember, we parted on *very* friendly terms.'

The slight tickle of her breath halted.

He looked down at her lips and then back to her eyes and they were both beyond turned on. His eyes then drifted down. Her nipples were erect and Matteo could smell the scent they made and he told her the truth. 'I could take you now and I wouldn't even have to pay you.'

She gave him the slowest smile. 'Of course you wouldn't have to pay me. I would do you for free, Matteo.' She dropped her voice from low to a throb. 'Do you want me in my uniform? That's very tame. Do you want a personal turn-down service or would you prefer to wake up to me? The choice is all yours.'

His fists bunched to hear her speak like that.

'Are you going to hit me again, Matteo?'

'Don't twist what happened then to suit you now.'

'I'm not.' Bella smiled wantonly. 'But you must know that if he is gentle, if he is considerate then a woman always has a soft spot for her first...' As the duty manager knocked on the door of the suite she continued her soft taunt. 'A tender spot...' Bella said. 'A sweet, warm spot...' And then she told him a truth of his own. 'Were you thinking of me as she sucked you?' Bella asked, and laughed out loud. 'But of course you were—I assume that you got my bed-side note, warning that tomorrow would be stormy and hot.'

'Jealous, Bella?' Matteo demanded, as there was another knock on the door to the suite. 'Is that the reason you threw water over us...?' He released her arm to go and get the door as she spoke on with a sneer in her voice.

'I wasn't jealous at all—my mother used to do the same to dogs in the street.'

He had been about to let the manager in but instead he turned and fronted her, his anger pushing her up against the wall.

'Shandy and I are not dogs and we were not out on the street. I was in bed with my lover...'

It was Bella's turn to be doused but it felt as if it was by acid as Matteo shrugged off the sheet and picked up his robe.

His words made her face go pale and she shrank against the wall. It hurt so much to hear that and the enormity of what she had done was just starting to hit.

And then she glimpsed again his beauty.

He wasn't bashful, there was no point, there was nothing of him that Bella hadn't already seen, and so as he dressed she was taunted by one last glimpse of Matteo Santini naked.

One glimpse was enough to reveal that his thighs were more muscular, his arms just as toned. One glimpse was too much for she saw him, half-aroused, lifting from his thigh, and she knew it would never be hers to hold again.

Matteo strode off to let the manager in and the angry blonde came out of the bathroom. Her hair was wrapped in a towel and Bella could not bring herself to look at her.

'Your maid…' Shandy shouted, as she brushed past Bella and into the lounge room, loudly voicing her complaint. 'She has completely ruined our morning…'

Matteo glanced over as Bella came through—the witch who had been in the bedroom had now turned her expression from seductive to contrite. Hell, she even managed to produce tears.

He could never have guessed that they were real.

'I said that I was sorry,' Bella attempted.

'Oh, it's way too late for that,' Shandy shouted, and then turned to Alfeo, the duty manager. 'Fire her.'

'There's no need for that,' Matteo said, and then he cleared his throat. 'It was an accident.' He was used to putting out fires, massive ones, yet it was taking everything he had to put out this tiny one and to treat Bella as if he didn't know her. 'It was a simple accident,' he reiterated, 'and no one got hurt.'

'Your maid *threw* a bucket of water over us!' Shandy shrieked. 'She didn't just trip, she actually took aim. This is going to hit the papers if I have my way. Do you have any idea who I am?'

The duty manager couldn't care less that Charlotte

Havershand, or Shandy as she preferred to be known, was the daughter of some English politician. His concern was more for Matteo Santini's reaction. Alfeo well knew that he was, along with his business partner Luka Cavaliere, considering purchasing this hotel. The room had been meticulously prepared, the staff had all been fully briefed and told that all the stops were to be pulled out for this most esteemed guest.

Alfeo knew too a little of Santini's dark past and so he swallowed nervously as he weighed his options. Yes, Santini might appear to be being reasonable but he had meted out many a silent punishment in the past and so Alfeo came to a rapid decision.

'You're fired,' Alfeo said to Bella.

'Alfeo…' Bella's tears were flowing now. 'Alfeo, please…'

'Go and wait in my office and I will give you your papers.'

'Alfeo…' Bella begged. 'I've worked here for five years and with one mistake you would—'

'Out!' Alfeo snapped, and with a sob she fled.

She offered no final plea to him, Matteo noted.

No parting shot either.

She simply turned and fled.

He should feel relief that she was gone.

He should snap to attention and resume the perfect life he had created but instead he just stared at the door she had run out of as the duty manger attempted to right her wrongs. 'Now, I will attend to the mess she has made myself but first, please, take a seat and I will have breakfast brought to you here in the lounge. I cannot apologise enough—'

'There was no need to fire her,' Matteo said, and

then he looked at Shandy, who was smirking as she sat down. 'You just cost someone their job. Does that not bother you?'

'What bothers me,' Shandy retorted, 'is that I have to get my hair done now when I was hoping to go shopping this morning. I do love the shops here…' she examined her nails, no doubt, Matteo thought, toying between coral or nude. He recalled Bella's bitten ones, as, despite his best attempts, the past finally, fully invaded, he could not live the lie a moment longer.

Breakfast was promptly delivered but Matteo waved away the new maid that had been sent and he also asked Alfeo to leave but said he would like to speak with him later, before he dealt with Bella.

He poured the coffee with a completely steady hand and as he did so Matteo dismissed his latest lover from his life.

Shandy didn't go quietly, but he was more than used to that.

She pleaded, she sobbed and the room was slightly trashed again, but finally Shandy was in his company jet and on the way back to London as Matteo sat in a hotel that Bella had given five years of her working life to.

Five years.

Matteo had assumed that her arrival here had been recent, a year or two perhaps.

Five years, though, must mean that she had left Bordo Del Cielo around the same time that he had.

It made no sense.

Matteo called for the duty manager to come up to discuss the morning's events.

'It really is most irregular,' Alfeo said, once Matteo had invited him to take a seat. 'We only have our best staff working on the top floors.'

'And Bella is one of your best?' Matteo checked.

'She's one of our more experienced staff,' Alfeo flushed.

'You've had problems with her before?' Matteo pushed. He had worked in hotels for a long time and knew when the duty manager was being evasive.

'Not problems as such…' Alfeo ran a worried hand through his hair and Matteo wondered if the manager's sudden discomfort possibly had something to do with his maid's extra-curricular activities. 'Despite our best preparations for your visit, it would seem there was a mix-up with the staff rosters. Bella doesn't usually work the top floors.'

Matteo was quite sure there had been no mix-up, he was quite sure that Bella had been busy meddling.

'I don't want her fired,' he said. 'You are to give her a warning but tell her that she has a second chance…' Matteo hesitated. 'After I check out, though. I leave here on Sunday for Dubai. Once I've gone, she can resume work.'

'Of course,' Alfeo said. 'You can tell your fiancé that she has nothing to worry about, she shan't be seeing Bella again—'

'That's all,' Matteo said, choosing not to correct Alfeo.

Shandy wasn't the problem.

With Bella in the same building, it was Matteo's willpower that might not hold out.

But it would not prove so easy to avoid her, Matteo found out just as the manager left and he took a call from Luka.

'It would seem you were right with what you said last night,' Luka sighed. 'Sophie has told her father that we will marry in Bordo Del Cielo this weekend…'

'And you said yes?'

'I told her that she had better hope that her father dies before the service on Sunday. I will go through the motions and make the right noises but it is all just a charade. No way will I go through with a marriage just to appease her father.'

'Finally you are speaking sense.'

'Will you be there?' Luka asked, and Matteo was about to say that he would but then Luka spoke on. 'One problem, though—Sophie is going to ask Bella Gatti to be bridesmaid.'

Matteo remembered getting to the airport, Luka waiting. He remembered his tension as he'd looked out for Bella and her mother, ready to explain them if they showed.

They hadn't.

And so he hadn't told Luka that he had planned to take Bella with him.

But Luka had heard from a couple of people about that last wild night in Bordo Del Cielo.

'I just wanted to warn you in case it makes things awkward for you and Shandy. Will you be there?' Luka asked again.

'I shall be,' Matteo said. 'I'm not sure about Shandy, though.' For reasons of his own he did not, even to his friend, reveal that he and Shandy were over.

'We're flying out early Saturday,' Luka said.

'I'll make my own way,' Matteo said. 'I have an appointment that morning, but I can only stay till the Sunday evening, though. I have to get to Dubai.'

'Can you reschedule that? Given that I'm not going to go through with the wedding it's going to be a helluva mess. It would be good if you could—'

'Sorry. I can't.'

Matteo hung up the phone.

Of course he could have rescheduled but it was safer not to.

He had kept her away for the next few days.

It would be impossible after that.

Oh, before the wedding there would be plenty to keep them busy, but by the Sunday night…

Even if it meant letting down his best friend, Matteo would not be staying for Luka's wedding night.

He wanted one more time with Bella.

But that would be foolish at best.

CHAPTER THREE

BELLA SAT IN Alfeo's office, chewing her nails.

She could not afford even a single day without work. Most of her savings had been depleted helping Sophie to face Luka.

The rest she kept for herself—Bella did not consider it her money to spend. It was to go towards giving her mother a headstone for her grave, for she had heard that Malvolio had made sure Maria had received a pauper's funeral.

But it wasn't just that she might be about to lose her job that had Bella anxious and close to tears.

It was seeing Matteo again.

The vision of him with his fiancée still danced before her eyes. His use of the word *lover* for another woman had, despite brave, taunting words to him, shaken Bella to her very core.

She loathed his beauty, his arrogance and his passion. She loathed everything about him if it was not aimed at her.

Sure, she had read about his many women over the years.

It had been hell, though, seeing it with her own eyes.

Yes, she had engineered this morning.

Even though she'd known he had booked for two, Bella knew how short-lived his relationships were and had hoped against hope that she might find him alone. In the little fantasy that her mind had created, the agony of finding him with another woman, and intimately too, had not been properly factored in.

No, tipping the water over Matteo and his lover had been no accident.

'Bella.'

She stood when Alfeo entered but he gestured for her to sit down.

'I am sorry about this morning,' Bella started. 'In five years of service there have been no incidents…'

Alfeo wasn't so sure about that! 'What about the dress that went missing that time and was found in your locker?'

Bella's teeth ground together. 'The guest had put the dress in the bin.'

'And the same guest called Housekeeping a few hours later to say that she had changed her mind and could we go through the garbage…'

Bella pulled a face…typical of the clientele here that they would have the staff rummage through garbage on a whim.

'I gave you the benefit of the doubt that time,' Alfeo said, and Bella did her best not to roll her eyes. She had been given the benefit only because she'd known that items tossed aside by wealthy guests all too often found their way into Alfeo's locker.

'What about the perfume that went missing earlier this week?'

'I spilt that.'

'Straight into a little decanter,' Alfeo said, and Bella met his eyes and lied.

'No.'

She had stolen just the little she'd needed, enough to fill the vial in her mother's heavy crystal bottle, the one her father had given to Maria.

Bella was a survivor and she wasn't too proud to take from bins if it meant she could keep her dress-making dreams alive, and thank God that she had because she had been able to fashion an elegant ward-robe for Sophie. And, yes, she had taken a smudge of perfume from a huge bottle but that was so Sophie could go to Luka smelling as she deserved to.

'You remind me of a magpie, Bella. If it glitters, if it catches your beady eyes, then you want it,' Alfeo said, but as Bella opened her mouth to argue he got to the point. 'But all that aside, what happened this morning defies logic. The ice bucket stand was still standing, yet you say that you tripped and knocked it over.'

'I wasn't aware that you were re-creating a crime scene.' Bella struggled to hold her tongue.

'It might just as well be a crime scene! How the hell do I explain this in a report? Matteo Santini is looking to buy this place. We are trying to show the hotel in its very best light and you choose to give our most important guests a morning bed bath. What the hell were you thinking?'

She gave in then. Given what had happened, there was no way she could keep her job.

'Can I at least have a reference?' Bella asked.

'Saying what? That Bella Gatti is a liar when she chooses to be, as well as an occasional thief...'

'You could always say that Bella Gatti is a hard worker,' Bella argued. 'That she works ten-hour days and often stays well past that, all without complaint.'

'Or I could tell you that Bella Gatti is on her final warning,' Alfeo said, and he put her out of her misery. 'I've just come from speaking with Mr Santini. He was most insistent that he does not want you fired but has asked that you take leave for the remainder of this week. I doubt he wants his fiancée to know that he has spared you,' Alfeo said. 'He checks out on Sunday, so you can resume work the next day.'

She sat there, completely stunned, as Alfeo spoke on.

'Bella, know that I'm watching you. I still don't believe this morning was an accident.'

She gave no smart answer. Instead, she thanked Alfeo for the reprieve.

'Bella…' Alfeo halted her as she stood to leave. 'I don't know why a guest of his standing would take such a personal interest in one of the maids…'

'Perhaps he is just kind,' Bella said, but there was a blush creeping from her throat to her cheeks.

'From everything I have heard and read about him, Matteo Santini is not a kind man. He doesn't give out favours,' Alfeo said, and then he was blunt. 'Do you?'

'I don't…I don't know what you mean,' Bella stammered.

'Oh, but I think you do,' he said, and then he warned her clearly. 'If I ever find out that you are having intimate dealings with our guests…'

'I'm insulted that you would suggest such a thing,' Bella said, but her cheeks were still pink because had Matteo been alone…

'Then I apologise.'

She headed out through the back entrance into the alley and then she saw Matteo leaning against a wall. Long limbed, elegantly dressed, his expression utterly unreadable, she wanted to run to him. Had he stretched out his arms or even beckoned a finger she might well have done that, but then she remembered he had someone, that Matteo was, in fact, engaged.

He was, Bella thought, far too beautiful for an alley.

So was she, Matteo decided as she walked towards him.

'What happened with the duty manager?' Matteo asked.

'I think you already know—I get to keep my job, though of course not while you are here with your fiancée.' She closed her eyes and tried to breathe through the surly note to her voice and to remember her place for he might soon be her boss. 'Thank you.'

Matteo looked at her pinched nostrils and knew the effort behind those two words and he could not help but smile.

'What is there to smile about?' she challenged.

'Plenty,' Matteo said, which had Bella frowning.

There was not a lot to smile about, Matteo thought, but there was enough—they were here.

'Do you want to go for breakfast?' Matteo offered, and it completely took Bella by surprise.

'Why?' she asked. 'Won't your fiancée…?'

Matteo had already decided that it might be safer not to reveal to Bella that he and Shandy had broken up, or that they had never been engaged—he hadn't needed to see Bella again for memories to try and make themselves known.

He had offered her his world and she had rejected it.

Want was still there, though.

No, it was far safer for him to keep a fiancée in the wings when she was around.

'Surely two friends are allowed to catch up.' Matteo took a breath. 'I want to know how you are.'

She wanted to know how he was too and so she nodded but then looked down at what she was wearing—she had taken off her apron but the pale green dress and flat lace-up shoes were far from flattering. 'I'm not dressed for—'

'It's only breakfast.' Matteo shrugged. 'But, sure, let's go to your home so you can change.'

Bella gave a tight shrug and then walked alongside him.

He was perfection. In a gorgeous suit, with not a glimmer of sweat on his brow despite the bright morning sun. He slipped on dark glasses when they stepped out of the alley and Bella did the same. Only hers were cheap ones and did little against the glare, but she wore them so he could not see the tears in her eyes.

Oh, it was hard to see him so sleek and beautiful. Harder too to get out of her head the image of him in bed this morning with a woman that had not been her.

'You share an apartment with Sophie?' Matteo checked.

'I do.' Behind her glasses Bella blinked nervously. For Sophie's sake she did not want Matteo to see how they really lived—they had done all they could to avoid the embarrassment.

For her sake too now, Bella thought.

'Sophie told Luka that you worked from home.'

There was a slight inference there and, given her

behaviour this morning and the way she had spoken to him, Matteo clearly thought she was topping up her wages with the oldest profession in the world.

Once a whore...

She recalled his words.

Bella knew what she had done to get here to Rome and she knew he would never forgive that.

He didn't need to know the salacious details and certainly Bella never wanted to tell him.

In some ways it was easier to go along with his thinking, to be smart-mouthed and streetwise.

To pretend that facing him wasn't the hardest thing she had ever done.

She glanced up at Matteo. He was so effortlessly elegant, so out of place by her side.

Yet, just as she always had, she loved him.

'Wait here,' Bella said.

'You're not going to invite me into your home?'

'No.'

'That's not very Sicilian,' Matteo teased lightly.

'Ah, but we are in Rome,' Bella said. 'You know how city people are, peeking out from behind their door, terrified you might want to come in.'

'I do.'

'Well, you can't,' she said. 'I won't be long.'

She left him at the end of her street.

The buildings were high, and some of the ancient buildings contained apartments that had been beautifully renovated. He could not guess, Bella hoped, that hers was not.

She turned down another small side street, unlocked a huge iron security gate and wrenched it back, and then climbed the many steps that led to a very small apartment.

Their lounge was relatively spacious but bare. It easily held two small sofas and a coffee table. Off that was a kitchen and Bella headed straight to the fridge and took out a bottle of water and drank it down, but nothing was going to help her become cool and sophisticated this morning. All their combined efforts had gone into ensuring that Sophie could present herself to Luka looking chic and glamorous—Sophie had wanted to appear far from the peasant that Luka had admitted to calling her during the trial.

Had she given it proper thought, Bella might have known that if Luka was around, then Matteo would be too.

But you deliberately didn't think, Bella reminded herself.

For five years she had done everything she could to keep the memories out.

Now he was back and the best she could do was pull from her drawer a small black tube skirt and add to it a tight top with spaghetti straps.

She ran a cloth over black ballet pumps and then brushed and retied her hair and headed out, locking the iron gate behind her. She walked back up the narrow hilly street to where he waited.

'That was quick,' Matteo said.

'Did you want me to make a little more effort for you?'

'I meant,' he said as they walked, 'that that was quick.'

There was tension between them.

Bella was still furious at the sight that had greeted

her this morning and Matteo had been less than impressed by her crude seductive taunt.

But aside from that there was a different tension, once-upon-a-time lovers trying to act as polite, distant friends who were merely catching up and wondering how the hell to adapt to that.

'How about here?' Matteo suggested as, instead of a corner café he stopped by a fashionable restaurant, and Bella nearly turned and ran.

She had once tried to apply for a waitressing job at this very restaurant and hadn't even made it past the doorman.

She knew that she wasn't glossy enough even to wait on tables here, let alone sit at them, but Matteo was already asking for a pavement table.

She saw a couple of sideway glances—and she knew they were for him. Here amongst Rome's elite and most beautiful he still stood out.

The frowns, though, the double takes, well, they were for her.

Amongst Rome's elite and most beautiful Bella stood out, but for all the wrong reasons.

They took their seats and as the waiter arranged the shade cloth, for once Bella thought Rome looked beautiful.

'How do you find Rome?' Matteo asked.

'Busy,' she said.

'Do you miss home?'

'This is home,' she said, glad for dark glasses. 'What about you—do you miss Bordo Del Cielo?'

'No.' Matteo shook his head. 'I have nothing there to miss.'

'Your mother?' she asked.

'She and her new husband moved away after Malvolio died. The property prices went up and they sold out. They spent all the money they made, of course...' He didn't elaborate, he was tired of his mother's dramas.

'Do you keep in touch?'

'She rings for money, I send it. That's it.'

'You don't see her?'

He gave a very brief shake of his head.

'Do you ever wonder about her?' Bella asked, though the lump in her throat meant she was asking more about herself.

'I don't let myself,' he said.

'What about your brother, Dino?' Bella asked, and she watched his jaw tense. She knew what Dino had told him about her.

'Dino is in prison. Once Malvolio died there was no one who wanted his ways. He is in the same prison that Paulo was.'

'Do you visit him?'

'No,' Matteo said. 'I do everything I can not to think of him.' He shrugged. 'I'm sure he's the same, people don't change.'

'They don't,' Bella said. The poor stay poor, she thought. The rich get richer and the beautiful age well.

She looked at the living proof.

There he was, immaculate and completely at ease.

And there was her image in his glasses and when she saw that she was nibbling on her nails she moved them from her mouth and sat a little straighter.

'Do you like your work?' he asked.

'Oh, I love to make beds.' Bella's voice dripped sarcasm. 'And sometimes, when I am shining a sink,

I feel so blessed, but that doesn't compare to cleaning a rich drunk's toilet.'

'What about your dressmaking?'

'What about it?' She shrugged. 'I am not as good as I thought I was. I have applied to many design schools…'

'You don't need a design school,' he said. 'You could start up now.'

Behind her glasses Bella's eyes narrowed—clearly he did not understand that even buying fabric proved hard, that she worked ten- or twelve-hour shifts at the hotel just to stay afloat. Alfeo was wrong—she wasn't some magpie, she didn't crave nice things, she just ached to make them, to bite her scissors into fabric, to create, to sew, but that was a dream that was fast fading. 'You have never seen my work.'

'I saw it last night,' Matteo said. 'Sophie was wearing one of your creations. She pretends to be rich…'

Bella's breath tripped. She and Sophie had done everything they could so that she could be proud of herself when she asked Luka to do her this one favour.

'I know that she lies,' Matteo said, and it was the strangest thing because even with the most private of conversations, even with her best friend's secret on her shoulders, there was somehow trust that the discussion taking place was between them.

'Does Luka know that she lies?'

'I don't know,' Matteo admitted. 'We really don't speak about our pasts. All I know is that Sophie contacted him and asked him to go along with a fake engagement to appease her father. Now she wants marriage.' His lips curled a little. 'I have warned him it will be an expensive divorce.'

'This isn't about money,' Bella swiftly retorted. 'This is about giving Paulo peace in his final days.'

'We shall see.' Matteo shrugged. 'Why else would she lie and make out that she is wealthy?'

'Perhaps she needed to feel some pride to look an ex-lover in the eye and ask for help,' Bella said from behind her dark glasses.

'Anyway,' he said, 'whatever game Sophie is playing, if what she was wearing last night was one of the dresses you made, then your work is amazing.'

'It would take just one beautiful woman to make the headlines wearing one of my gowns.' A smile finally came to her face. 'Perhaps you could ask Shandy to wear one at one of the functions you attend…'

'I don't think so.' Matteo's own smile was wry. The waiter came and Bella glanced through the menu as he ordered a *panino*.

'Brioche with a side of pistachio and cherry gelato,' she said.

'That sounds a lot like home,' he commented.

'I don't eat out a lot,' Bella said. 'And so, when I do, I want something that I know for sure I'll like.'

Her words hit him between the legs. She could make the water the waiter was pouring a reference to sex, he thought as Bella excused herself and walked into the restaurant.

There was no need to be shy now. As Matteo Santini's breakfast date, the door was held open.

A machine in the wall offered various solutions and normally Bella wouldn't even deign to give it a glance.

Today wasn't a normal day, though, and so she fed some coins in.

Some splurge, Bella thought as half a milligram of lip gloss was delivered to her palm.

She painted her mouth, she rearranged her top, she tried to breathe through the images that her mind kept delivering.

Their first kiss, their one dance.

She took her time but felt better for it and as she walked back out the waiter was already returning with her order.

Matteo could have kicked himself for bringing her here. He could see a group of women look down at her shoes and then whisper something.

All he had thought since their eyes had met this morning was how amazing she looked. Now, thanks to others, he could see that her little black skirt was a little faded, that her shoes were scuffed and that her amazing black hair was split and could use a good cut. It had never been his intention to place her under public scrutiny and yet he had done just that.

Here, looks mattered, clothes mattered, down to the bag you carried and the sunglasses you wore.

She thanked the waiter as she sat down and he wished he could take her hand and tell her not a scrap of it mattered to him. She, above everyone he knew, must know his thoughts on all that.

Because that long-ago night he had told her.

Bella slit the bread open and scooped the gelato into it and closed her eyes as she took a bite, and when she saw Matteo watching her she sliced her bread into two and handed him half and they spoke a little of Bordo Del Cielo.

'I hear it is busy now, that the tourists come to the hotel,' Bella said. 'Too many of them apparently, though the people are much happier now that Malvolio is dead.'

'We will see for ourselves at the weekend,' Matteo responded, and he watched as the bread paused by her mouth.

Bella didn't even attempt a bite. Instead, she put the food down. 'What do you mean—we'll see for ourselves at the weekend?'

'Sophie hasn't spoken to you yet?' Matteo checked.

'No.'

'I got a phone call this morning. She and Luka have booked their wedding for Sunday and I am to be the best man. I have heard that Sophie shall ask you to be bridesmaid.'

'I'm working,' Bella said quickly, her mind dancing with the news. Luka had been adamant that he would never marry Sophie and she wanted to hear from her friend exactly what was going on.

'No,' he reminded her. 'You're not working, remember.'

'Is that why you said I couldn't start back till Monday?'

Any hope that he wanted her there, that he had somehow arranged things so that she might be in Bordo Del Cielo for the wedding, were immediately removed by a rather adamant shake of his head.

'I heard about the wedding after I spoke with your manager.'

'So your efforts to keep me from Shandy will be in vain.' Bella gave a hollow laugh. 'She'll get a surprise when she sees me at the wedding. Perhaps she will throw a bucket of water over us when we dance...'

Matteo didn't correct Bella and tell her that Shandy

wouldn't be there. Instead, he outlined how it would be. 'Ah, but we will be behaving,' Matteo said, while knowing it was close to an impossible task.

He wondered if he should tell her not to worry about a dance that would possibly kill them both but he chose to leave it to Sophie to tell her that the wedding would not be going ahead.

They sat silent for a moment and then, aching to see her, Matteo reached over and took off the dark glasses that hid her eyes.

Bella let him.

'You look tired,' he commented.

'Because I am tired,' she said. 'And I am uncomfortable here too. People keep looking at us.'

Matteo said nothing, he couldn't deny that people were.

'I don't like the scrutiny,' she said.

Matteo called for the bill.

CHAPTER FOUR

ROME WAS SO beautiful today, Bella thought as they stepped out into the sun.

There were tourists and lovers and all the scents of a city and how strange it felt to be here with Matteo and not to be holding hands.

Not to be pressed up against a wall this hot morning and kissing with all the promise of later falling into bed.

'Not a cloud…' Matteo looked up. 'I thought your note said there would be storms.'

'I'm the storm.' Bella smiled and so did he.

'I did some sightseeing last night,' he said, and she gave him a sideways frown because she couldn't really imagine Matteo doing such a thing. 'I hired a moped and—'

'I don't want to hear about your night with Shandy.'

'I wasn't with her then,' Matteo said. 'I was with you.'

He stopped walking and so did she and they faced the other but stood apart.

'We could do that together now,' he said. 'I could hire a moped, we could—'

'No,' Bella said.

'But you told me that you love exploring.'

'I do.'

'So why not?' Matteo pushed, but when she gave her answer he wished that he hadn't.

'Because then we'd be touching.'

They walked, not talking, just together, and then came to a grassy knoll where families sat and so too did couples.

Matteo bought two coffees and they sat there, watching the world go by. Tired from a night spent thinking of each other, they lay on the grass and Bella took off her glasses and let the warm sun bathe her.

If there was one place in the world where Bella felt she belonged, it was lying by his side. There, she could look up and see no one and feel no one watching or, if she looked to the side, she could see only him.

Matteo, still in dark glasses, was looking up at the sky as she turned to him and gazed at his perfect straight nose and strong profile.

'I do miss home.' He admitted to his lie in the restaurant. 'Not the people, more…' He hesitated.

'I miss it too,' she said. 'Every day I tell myself that I love Rome and I do. I love the freedom, I love that I am no longer scared, yet I miss so many things about Bordo Del Cielo. I miss the beach,' she admitted. 'Sophie and I would go there every day. I miss the markets too and the food. I miss days spent exploring. If I lived there for ever there would still be more to discover…'

'How was your mother about you leaving?' Matteo asked.

Bella lay there.

Because she had so few people in her life, the question barely came up. She had only had to say perhaps a handful of times that her mother was dead, and she just didn't know how to say it now and not break down.

She asked him a question instead.

'What do you miss?'

'I don't know exactly. Just those last six months…' Matteo answered. He took no offence that she hadn't answered; he was the master at being evasive when people asked things about his past.

He thought for a moment and she watched, a little smile on his dark red lips as he thought of them. 'I've never even told Luka, given he spent those months in prison, but during that time, running the hotel not having someone breathing down my neck, I felt I might get somewhere, I could see myself living there without wanting to get away…'

'Do you really not miss your mother?' Bella asked. She just couldn't imagine he wrote his family off that easily.

'There's nothing to miss. She was barely there when I was growing up. She hated me,' Matteo said, and Bella frowned.

'I doubt she actually hated you…'

'Oh, she told me so,' he said. 'And he didn't have to tell me that, his fists did the talking. I never remember a time she wasn't married to him…' Even to this day Matteo would not call his stepfather by name.

'Do you think she might have been scared to show him she loved you?'

'Perhaps at first but then she became as cruel as him. I remember when I was about five and I sat there at the dinner table and, as always, she served him first. Then she served Dino, he would have been about three, then she served herself. I remember watching her. I was hungry, but then *he* said he wanted more sauce on his pasta and so she gave him more. Then Dino. Always. I knew the routine and only after they had had seconds would she serve me. But that time she didn't. She served more for herself and I got not only the scraps, I got the message—I came nowhere.'

Bella could remember her own mother and how she would tell her she had already eaten, how she'd done everything she could to make sure that Bella didn't go hungry.

To think that a mother would do that deliberately.

'I would go to Luka's. I didn't like it much there either but there was always food. I was home less and less but then Luka went to boarding school so I had no choice but to go back. We had a row when I was fifteen and I haven't spent a night there since.'

'Was that when she told you she hated you?'

'Yep,' Matteo said. 'Or rather, I asked her why she hated me and she said that I reminded her of my father. I didn't really know much about him so I said, "What, did he treat you badly?" She said no, he had treated her well and that was why she could not stand to look at me. I was too painful a reminder of good times.'

'Where did you go?'

'Malvolio said I could stay in one of the fisherman's cottages on the beach. I told him I couldn't pay rent and he said that was no problem. He would find some jobs for me.' Behind his glasses Matteo rolled his eyes. 'And of course he did. I used to resent Luka. He went and studied in London and I wanted to ask if

I could go and join him but I was too proud. I made
out that I loved the place... When he came back to
end things with Sophie, I knew he was cutting all ties.
We were going to meet up for a drink at the airport.
I was going to ask him then to help me get out but,
like you, he never showed. He had an excuse, though,
given he'd been arrested...'

She didn't take the opening.

'What's your excuse, Bella? Were you never intending to show, or did Maria talk you out of it?'

Still she did not answer him.

'Tell me another truth, then,' Matteo said, and he
did not turn his head to hers. 'This morning wasn't
an accident.'

'No.'

'Did you plan to throw the water?'

'Do you really want the truth?' Bella checked,
and now their faces turned and Matteo removed his
glasses and their eyes met. 'I hoped you might be
alone.'

'To talk?' he asked.

'No,' Bella said. 'I find talking to you the hardest part...' She thought back to last night and the little note she had written him. There had been this
tiny kernel, a tiny dream that with Sophie and Luka
together, even temporarily, Matteo might have been
hoping to see her too.

'So what would have happened if I had been alone?'
Matteo asked.

If you could be unfaithful with just your eyes, he
was then.

And if you could be the other woman with just a
look, then that was who she was.

They did not touch, their eyes did not assess each other's bodies but, Bella knew, if he was hers and he shared this look with another woman, she would die.

He looked down at her mouth and there was such tension in her lips as they fought from meeting his and then he moved back to her gaze.

They made love.

Past love, perhaps, but together they watched the memory. He bathed her, washed her, tasted her, made love to her and they both lay, five years later, locked in recall.

It was such a dangerous game they played with their eyes.

'We were so good,' she murmured.

'We were.'

And if they moved, even a fraction, they could not justify to anyone that they were mere friends.

'But you have a nice life now…' Bella tried to break the spell. 'I see you in some of the magazines.'

'They make a lot of stuff up.'

'And they tell some truths,' she said. 'They found out about your scar. You never told me you were stabbed.'

'I said to you that I was in a fight.'

'And it was interesting to read that Shandy got suspended from school when she was sixteen for drinking.'

Matteo swallowed. His throat was suddenly dry; he knew what was coming.

'They pay a lot of attention to your past, don't they?'

'Yes.'

'Then it is just as well that we're not together because they would have a field day with mine,' she said. 'I remember that you said, you would hate my past to bring you down.'

'Bella—'

'But aside from your embarrassment about me and my past and perhaps my mother, I could not stand to be discussed like that by the press, Matteo.'

'I know.'

'I would not want the scrutiny.'

Bella stood up then. It was easier to walk and keep her distance, to remind herself why she could never belong by his side.

They walked and then sat on the Spanish Steps, still not touching, back safe behind dark glasses, even though she knew the questions were going to come.

'You said to your manager that you had worked at the hotel for five years...' There was a slight huskiness to Matteo's voice, a rare nervous edge as they approached the most difficult of subjects. 'That would mean you came to Rome soon after...' He didn't finish the sentence.

'Nearly three months after...' Bella said, not completing it either—they both knew they were discussing that night and the plans that had been made that morning. 'My mother had a stroke that morning. I came home and found her on the floor. She died three months later.' Bella could see the shock in his expression. After all, Maria had only been thirty-four when she'd died. 'Did you never think to find out why I wasn't there?'

'I gave you money to leave...' Matteo said, and then let out a tense breath as he looked back on the time. 'I spoke with Dino a few weeks after I left. He never mentioned that your mother was sick. He said you were enjoying working in the bar, that he was enjoying…' He couldn't finish the sentence. Even now the thought of Dino with Bella made him feel ill.

'Your brother is a liar,' she said. 'Haven't you worked that out yet? I never set foot in the bar after that night with you. On the night before my mother's funeral, just after Paulo's sentencing, I ran away to Rome and because of that she lies in a pauper's grave.'

'Bella—'

'I got to Rome. Sophie had found a flat and…' She hesitated. As honest as she had been, she chose not to tell him that Sophie had been working at the hotel when she had arrived. That was for Sophie to share with Luka if ever she chose to. 'I got a job as a chambermaid at Hotel Fiscella and I've been there ever since.'

'So you haven't…' He didn't quite know how to voice it and Bella got up then and walked away briskly. He came up behind her but she just kept right on walking till they stood at the Trevi Fountain. Tourists were jostling for position, throwing in coins in the hope they might one day return.

'Sometimes I think of the baths back home,' Bella said. 'You know they say that a young girl led Roman soldiers to a source of pure water…' She looked at the magnificent structure and still, magnificent as it was, the most famous fountain in the world, it wasn't home.

She went into her bag and took out a coin and kissed it but then, instead of throwing it in the fountain, she handed it to him and closed his fingers around it.

'Please put it in your pocket so that you don't come

back, Matteo. Let's get through this wedding but,
please, don't come back because if you do, if you
buy the hotel, I'll leave and I will have to start my life
over again when I'm tired of starting over.'

'Bella?'

She could not avoid it, there could be no more
changing the subject. It was here that she must face
her past because Matteo was turning her to look at
him as he addressed the painful topic of her *other*
line of work. 'Are you telling me that you never…' It
was still a sentence he could not finish. The thought
of her with Dino had made him vomit in the past, the
thought of her being used still made him feel ill and
so, when words failed, he took her hand, but that just
angered her.

'Oh, I pass your test now, do I? I'm suddenly re-
spectable because you were my only client?' She was
bitter, she was angry, but more than that she was so,
so ashamed of the very hand that he had tried holding that it actually burnt as she took it back. 'Well,
before you get your hopes up, know that I don't pass
your test, Matteo. Sometimes you do what you have
to to survive. It's not always pretty.'

'Bella…'

She didn't want to hear it, she didn't want to try
and justify things.

She was here.

With her shame perhaps.

But she was here and alive.

Even if it had cost any chance for them.

Bella did a terribly cruel thing then.

To herself.

She reached up and took off his glasses and even

if Matteo did his best to mask it, he didn't quite and she saw not just the disappointment there but something else.

Bella took it to be his disgust.

CHAPTER FIVE

BELLA LEFT HIM THEN.

She didn't want his attempts at a normal conversation after her revelation. She just wanted to be alone and so, without a further word, she tossed his glasses back at him and then pushed her way through the crowd and headed for home.

And Matteo let her go.

For Bella, the rest of the day was long and spent trying not to think of him so she chose to escape from her thoughts the best way she knew how.

She still couldn't quite take in the news that Sophie and Luka were to marry this Sunday.

She knew she would hear it first-hand soon but if it was true, if they really were about to wed, then there was one thing she could do other than pace their tiny apartment, trying not to dwell on a night that had taken place five years ago.

She went through to the small kitchen, knelt under the table and pulled out two bricks and then put her hand in.

Oh, she had done her best not to touch the money she had saved for her mother's stone but sometimes it was a matter of taking care of the living and Bella wanted to help her friend in the best way she knew how.

Bella headed to the market and to her favourite stall, where she spoke at length with the owner as she examined the bundles of fabric and the little boxes of beads.

'This is beautiful,' Bella said, running her hand over a length of ivory tulle that was affordable but they both knew she was trying to convince herself for her eyes kept going to the back of the stall and a roll of fabric that was close to four times the price of the one she was looking at. 'Let me see that one again,' she said.

It was chiffon, the texture similar to that of the engagement dress she had once made for Sophie, though that had been a cotton chiffon and this was in silk. And that had been coral. This, though, was a parchment white.

'It would be very difficult to work with,' Bella said, still trying to dissuade herself from spending so much, 'and I don't have much time.'

There would be no time for beading, Bella thought, but then again her best work had been the most simple cuts. And the challenge of working with such an exquisite fabric, to create for a relatively small price a dress that might cost thousands, even tens of thousands in a bridal store, had her heart beating with excitement.

The thought of making, with love, a wedding dress for her friend fulfilled a long-ago promise. Oh, Bella had thought she would be rich by then, a famous seamstress who people flocked to. She laughed for a moment, remembering sitting at their secret cove at home, looking out across the water. Bella would be rich and famous and Sophie was going to sail the seas, working on the cruise liners.

Life had seemed a lot simpler then.

She would do this for her friend, Bella decided. Even if the wedding was a fake one, Bella knew that Sophie's heart resided with Luka.

And, Bella knew, as the stallholder cut out the required length, this might be her one and only truly luxurious creation—she was snared in the poverty trap, sewing together other's cast-offs, whereas this would the first piece of clothing that she had made from scratch in years.

Bella bought oil for her small sewing machine and silk thread as well as needles and tissue paper and then raced home.

She set to work in the bedroom, cutting out the pattern from memory. Sophie was curvy, a little more full in the bust and hips than she had been at eighteen, but Bella allowed for that.

She ached to cut into the fabric but she forced herself to be patient. Measure twice, cut once wasn't going to work here, but at the very least she could get started on the skirt. Finally, that night, the first cut was made, her scissors slicing through the sheer fabric until the beginning of a dress was born—the fabric, like huge tulip petals, was still pinned to paper but its beauty was starting to emerge when she heard the rattle of the security gate and Sophie's voice.

'Sophie…'

Bella came out of the bedroom and hugged her teary friend as soon as she stumbled into the apartment.

'Luka says that he wished he'd never loved me,' Sophie sobbed, and she told Bella far more than Matteo had. 'He's going to jilt me.'

And though Bella would have loved to linger on her own problems, there were times when a friend, no matter how badly your own heart was bleeding, needed you to help with the gaping wound in theirs. Her own problems could wait for now, she decided.

Sophie was leaving tomorrow for Bordo Del Cielo to be jilted in front of the town, and to add to things her father was dying.

Yes, Bella put her own problems aside.

'I had an argument with my father,' Sophie wept. 'He wants me to wear my mother's wedding dress and I said no. I don't want a marriage like theirs.'

Never had Bella been happier to spend her savings for the smile she gave her friend then. 'I'm already making your wedding dress.' She told her that she would be working on it through the night. 'I'm going to be there with you, Sophie.'

'No.' Sophie shook her head. 'You have to work, and anyway…'

'Anyway?'

'Matteo will be there and…'

'I know that he has a woman,' Bella said. 'And I know that she is stunning. I'd love to come and be your bridesmaid, Sophie. And don't worry about work—as of this morning I am suspended.'

'Bella?'

'I got in a lot of trouble,' she explained with a slightly

mischievous smile. 'I spilt an ice bucket on a guest's lap when I was delivering the breakfasts to the room.'

'An ice bucket?'

'It was mainly cold water. I tripped but his girl-friend kicked up a fuss and called for the manager. It was a simple accident. The room was dark. I didn't see him—or rather they didn't hear me come in with breakfast. They were otherwise engaged.'

Sophie looked up at the sound of venom and mis-chief in Bella's voice and her mouth actually gaped for a moment before she spoke.

'You threw a bucket of iced water over Matteo?'

'I did.' Bella grinned. 'So, you see, now I am free to be at your wedding and I'm going to work on your wedding dress tonight. Sophie, you're going to be the most beautiful bride.'

She would be.

Bella took a lot of measurements as they chatted. Paulo's house had been part of Malvolio's estate and was now owned by Luka. 'He's given it back to my father,' Sophie said. 'Well, at least that is what he has said to him. Who knows what will happen when my father is dead? For now, though, it is good that he thinks he has a home.'

'I want to see my old home,' Bella said. 'I'm sure it has people living there now but I might knock and ask if they will let me come in, or at least take some cuttings from the garden. She loved her flowers so much.'

It was good to have her friend back in the apart-ment but a strained Sophie, now she had relaxed a

little and confided in her friend, could barely keep
her eyes open.

'Go to sleep,' Bella said.

'We fly at seven,' Sophie said. 'On his luxury jet.'

'So we will return to Bordo Del Cielo in style.'
Bella smiled. 'You just try and rest for now, we don't
want the bride to have bags under her eyes and ruin
my dress.'

Sophie smiled but then it changed into a yawn. 'Are
you nervous to see Matteo?' she asked.

'Not really,' Bella lied. 'We have already spoken.
He took me to some fancy restaurant for breakfast
this morning.' Bella gave a tight smile. 'He still thinks
I'm a whore.'

'I hope you put him right!'

Bella shook her head.

'Bella?'

'It was fine.' She squeezed her friend's hand. 'Don't
worry about me right now. We'll get through the next
few days, we've been through worse.'

'But you and Matteo…'

'Matteo and I can never be,' Bella said.

She hadn't even told her friend the full truth.

'But—'

'Get some sleep,' Bella interrupted. 'I don't want
to talk about Matteo now.'

She didn't want to think about him either.

She didn't want to look back at that time.

Neither did Matteo.

As Bella sat sewing, not far away Matteo was
speaking to his assistant, who had adjusted his itin-
erary. The company jet was being used by Luka so

he had had his assistant book his trips. Tomorrow mid-morning he was taking a helicopter to Bordo Del Cielo and it would bring him back to Rome at seven on the Sunday night and then he would fly to Dubai on Monday morning.

'One thing,' she checked. 'Will you be coming back to the same hotel on Sunday night?'

He was about to say no, but then remembered that Bella was to be a bridesmaid at the wedding that wasn't taking place.

No doubt she would be busy mopping up Sophie's tears.

'Yes,' Matteo said. 'For one night.'

Oh, he could have flown out of Bordo Del Cielo early on the Monday morning and still made his flight to Dubai, but there was safety in distance and he needed that distance from Bella.

He hung up the phone and told himself he didn't care about Bella. She had chosen that life, he reminded himself.

He had emptied not just his wallet that night, he had given her his heart, he had promised to take care of her, and she had thrown it all in his face.

Yes, he accepted her mother had been ill and that would account for her not being at the airport.

It didn't account for later, though.

Was it male pride that had let her walk off?

Was it her shameful past that had kept them apart?

It wasn't love he had found that night, it had been sex, that was all, he tried to tell himself.

Good sex.

But, no, he'd had plenty of that since then.

What had it been about that night that clung to him? A night that was as present as a damp cloud, seeping into everything, ensuring nothing was as bright or as clear as it had been then.

She was still beautiful, still slender and just as beguiling.

He wanted her.

Not just again. Matteo wanted Bella in his life.

No matter the others.

But, no, it wasn't just his ego and male pride that held him back.

She didn't want scrutiny and yet the press would make mincemeat of her, Matteo well knew.

They had a strange fascination with the dark, good-looking Italian who dated London's elite. It didn't quite sit right with them so they did their best to expose his past in any way they could.

They would expose hers, that much Matteo knew.

She would be named and shamed at every turn, her picture plastered everywhere, her mother's past played out, and there would not be a thing that Matteo could do about it.

Bella had struggled just to get through breakfast today. Imagine dropping her right into his world and the poison that would await.

He had to forget her, yet that one night stretched for a lifetime. One night with so many fragments, so many pieces, like little stars dropped into thoughts and dreams.

He could not fight it.

Yes, he had dreamt about it, recalled it in his sleep.

Now, awake, finally he allowed himself to fully remember. To recall in detail a time that, though long buried, refused to be laid to rest.

What he could not know was now, on the night before they returned to the town they had grown up in, Bella, who was making her friend's wedding gown, had put the garment down in her lap and stared unseeing as she recalled the beautiful and painful memories too.

CHAPTER SIX

Five years ago

THE PACKED COURTROOM smelt of wood oil, anticipation and fear.

The trial was over and the verdicts were about to come in and Bella looked down at her hand, which was holding Sophie's.

She had nails now.

Not long nails but they looked like tiny new moons on the ends of her fingers and that was what hope looked like, Bella thought.

With Malvolio behind bars, Matteo was in charge of the hotel, and under new management it had thrived.

Oh, she still worked long hours but there were two meal breaks now for the staff, with food provided. Hot chocolate and rolls for breakfast and usually pasta and sauce for lunch or supper, depending on the shift you were working. Louanna, the chef, would save a serving for Bella, which she would take home to her mother.

And so, instead of arriving home drained, hungry and exhausted, Bella would come home tired but, having warmed her mother's meal, there was still enough left in her tank to take out her sewing.

Matteo had said that the maids could keep their tips, which meant that the maids worked harder.

That was hope.

Bella could now buy fabric and she'd had her scissors sharpened.

She was starting to see a way out of the life she had been born into but, as she sat in the courtroom, Bella knew all that could end today.

'It will be okay,' she said to her friend as Luka stood to hear his fate.

It had to be okay. Luka had only returned to Bordo Del Cielo to break off his engagement with Sophie— the woman that he had been promised to since childhood.

Yet a police raid that evening, six months ago, had seen Luka, Malvolio and Paulo arrested.

Now he stood on trial for the sins of his father.

Surely, Bella thought, the judge would have seen that Luka had had nothing to do with Malvolio's dealings.

Bella let out a breath as Luka stood. As nervous as she was about the result, her eyes flicked, as they did all too often, to Matteo Santini.

His beautiful face was expressionless.

Matteo's suit was, as always, immaculate. Despite the heat in the courtroom his jacket was on and his tie beautifully knotted—not even the top button of his shirt was undone.

He looked as relaxed and vaguely bored as he might if he were waiting for a movie to start, Bella thought. One could never guess, if they didn't know, that he was waiting for the verdict about to be delivered on his closest friend.

Then again, Bella thought, was Matteo really close to anyone?

His dark eyes drifted around the room and came to rest on Sophie but then they moved to Bella and for a small second their gazes locked.

She blushed as she always did whenever Matteo was near, or when at work he had rare occasion to speak with her.

Not that he noticed, for already his eyes had left hers and had moved back to watch the verdict.

'Luka Romano Cavaliere—*non colpevole.*'

Matteo refused to blink but he could not help the sharp exhalation of breath as his best friend was found not guilty.

Thank God.

Luka was more a brother to him than Dino had ever been.

Matteo's father had died when he was young—old age was a rare treat in Bordo Del Cielo. By all accounts he had been a nice man but his mother had not chosen so well the next time.

Luka had never questioned the bruises on Matteo.

Just as Matteo had never questioned his.

Life was tough, even if, like Luka, your father owned the town.

Even if, like Matteo, you were the one who carried out Malvolio's wishes.

He glanced over to Sophie to see her reaction to the verdict. She and Luka had been caught in bed together and Luka had later stood in court and shamed her, had said that, despite his ending things, she had offered herself to him.

Sophie's eyes did not lift.

He glanced to the young woman beside her again, Bella Gatti.

Matteo knew who she was and not just from the times he had gone to her house to collect Maria's money. He had seen her at Brezza Oceana, of course, and he knew Sophie and Bella were friends, just like he and Luka were.

He looked at Bella more closely now and saw that her eyes were wide with fear, her skin was paler than usual, and she kept tucking her long black hair behind her ear in a nervous gesture as they now awaited Malvolio's verdict.

She looked petrified, Matteo realised, but, then, so too were most in the courtroom. Malvolio, if he was found not guilty, would be released and his reign of terror would start again.

Perhaps Bella was nervous for her mother.

Matteo knew that she was no longer working. She was racked with debt and soaked in alcohol, thanks to the man who was about to meet his fate.

Yes, that would account for Bella's nervousness, Matteo decided.

If Malvolio was released there would be debts to collect.

He did not relish the prospect in the least but surely Malvolio would not get off?

There was a hush in the courtroom and a moment of long-awaited jubilation was about to be born as the brute was finally brought to justice.

Malvolio stood.

Fat and sweaty, he dabbed at his forehead with a handkerchief and though Matteo silently prayed that he would be put away for life, he knew even that sentence could never atone for all the lives he had ruined.

How he hated that man, Matteo thought, saving the smile that wanted to spread on his lips for a moment from now.

'Malvolio Cavaliere—*non colpevole.*'

The courtroom was silent for just a few seconds too long at the shocking verdict, but it was as if everyone, in the next second, suddenly realised that Malvolio was back in charge of Bordo Del Cielo and frantic applause ensued.

Matteo did not join in, he just watched as Malvolio smirked.

He was back.

Matteo looked to where Malvolio's greedy gaze drifted and now he better understood Bella's look of fear.

No!

There was a moment of brief recall for Matteo—when he had first taken over management of the hotel he had checked the bar rosters and seen Bella's name.

He had scratched it out.

'No,' Matteo had said, because his intention was to clean up the bar. 'She is to keep working as a chambermaid.'

He would have no say now. Malvolio was free, and there was not a single thing he could do other than watch Bella sit and quietly weep.

And then Paulo stood.

He was Sophie's father and a weak, frail man. His wife, Rosa, had died when Sophie had been small.

By Malvolio's hand, Matteo was quite sure.

Matteo had worked alongside Paulo and had done some jobs that Paulo had either been too weak to do or could not bring himself to.

Though Matteo might appear to be Malvolio's yes-man, he quietly worked things his way.

As the court stood Matteo remembered a night a few years ago. Paulo had been told to burn down a house where a family slept and Matteo, returning from the bar, sent to check on him, had found Paulo sitting on a wall, holding a bottle of accelerant, his head in his hands.

'Talia was a friend of Rosa's,' Paulo wept. 'I cannot do this.'

'Then you are dead by tomorrow,' Matteo had said without emotion.

'Damn Malvolio.' Paulo for once had been strong. 'There are babies asleep in the house. I would rather be dead myself than do that.'

'Perhaps,' Matteo answered calmly. 'But what will happen to Sophie if you are not here to protect her? What will happen to your daughter if you are gone? Maybe Malvolio will find work for her. How old is she now?' Paulo's face bleached white and Matteo sat down on the wall beside him, a few steps away from where a family slept.

'Give it to me,' Matteo said, and took the bottle containing the accelerant. 'I'll take care of things. You go home, Paulo.'

'Matteo,' Paulo protested. 'I can't ask you to do my work for me.'

'Just go home,' Matteo said. 'I don't have anyone

that I need to take care of. No one worries about me and I have no one I need to worry for...'

It proved a blessing that night.

With Paulo gone, Matteo walked up to the small fisherman's cottage. Through the open window he could hear a baby crying and her mother singing, trying to get the infant back to sleep.

He should wait for the house to fall silent. Matteo knew all too well what to do.

But instead of waiting for the hush of silence, he went to the small room and knocked on the window, startling Talia, who went to shout out.

'Hush...' Matteo said, 'or you will get us all killed.'

She nodded wide-eyed and held in her scream.

'See this?' Matteo said, and she nodded as he held up the bottle.

'In five minutes' time fire will tear through your house, so go and get the babies and go out of the back door with your children...' As she went to go he halted her. 'Wait.'

Matteo picked up soil from the ground and smeared her tear-streaked face and then her hands, before Talia rushed off to gather up her precious babies.

A miracle, the villagers had called it.

Talia was a true heroine for somehow she had managed to get all her babies out in time.

Malvolio had shrugged. It had served as a warning to everyone. Whether they were dead or alive did not matter to him.

The next morning Paulo had met his eyes in brief thanks.

Matteo now glanced across the courtroom and there was Talia, the mother he had warned that night, and she gave him the tiniest smile, though he did not return it.

No one must ever guess what had happened back then.

Especially now that Malvolio would be walking the streets again.

The judge was calling for calm. The panicked people were still trying to take in that Malvolio would be back amongst them, Paulo for now was forgotten.

The other two had got off, no doubt he would too but then the courtroom was rocked again.

Paulo Durante—*colpevole*.

Paulo would be taken to the mainland for sentencing. The judge was calling for calm as people stood in the stands, shouting and raising their fists at the frail old man.

It was not justice that drove them to berate Paulo, it was fear of Malvolio.

As Matteo stepped out of the courtroom, despite the fierce sun in the bright blue sky it was a black day indeed.

As soon as Luka was processed and freed he came to talk to his friend.

Some things could not be discussed yet today they were.

'Matteo, I am going to speak with Sophie. Now that her father has been imprisoned her name too will be mud. I am leaving, I am not going to be my father's second in charge. I am taking Sophie to London with me.'

Matteo nodded and, though he didn't show it, he was surprised at Luka's honesty about his father, but nothing prepared him for what came next.

'You need to come with me.'

'Me?' Matteo said. He knew Malvolio would never allow it. He had already tried to leave once and, eternally mistrusting, he wasn't even sure that his friend wasn't calling his bluff—testing him as his brother once had. 'Why would I come with you? Nothing changes for me...'

'Everything changes,' Luka said, and Matteo felt his insides still. 'With me gone and Paulo about to be locked away, you will be my father's second man.'

'There is Dino,' Matteo said, referring to his half-brother, but Luka shook his head and Matteo could hear the blood pulsing in his temples as he realised that a distant heir, himself, had suddenly been promoted.

'There will be a lot of bloodshed to come,' Luka said, and Matteo knew then that he would be the one to exact Malvolio's revenge on those who had had the courage to speak out against him.

'We fly at nine tomorrow,' Luka said. 'If you tell anyone, well, you know what might happen, and not just to you. Think about joining us,' Luka said, and Matteo didn't respond, though his mind was busy as his friend spoke on. 'For tonight, just celebrate with my father, carry on as if you are thrilled that he has been released... He's watching your every move, Matteo. He doesn't believe you are completely loyal. Tonight you have to show him that you are, tonight you have to convince him that you want every part of his depraved lifestyle, or you and anyone you care for will be some of the forest that he is about to start clearing...'

'Then it is lucky I care for no one.'

Luka looked at his friend. 'Maybe this life is what you want,' he said, because even if they had a lot of history between them Matteo gave away little and no one really knew what went on in his mind. 'If it is then I wish you well, Matteo.'

'And you.'

'Even if you aren't going to join us, can you do one thing for me?'

Matteo nodded.

'Get him royally pissed so he sleeps like a bear through the morning.'

'Done.'

Luka walked away then and Matteo was in no doubt that he was heading off to try and persuade Sophie to join him.

Malvolio was processed through the court quickly and Luka had been right. It was clear that Matteo was now the go-to man—everyone was turning to him and asking what would be happening tonight.

'Perhaps a street party,' Matteo said. 'Everyone can see him that way and welcome his release.'

Matteo just wanted to keep him away from the bar and Bella.

He sat outside the jail house in his boss's car and shook Malvolio's hand in congratulations when he climbed in.

'What happens tonight?' Malvolio asked.

'A street party,' Matteo said. 'All the town wants to see you.'

'Am I ten years old?' Malvolio scoffed. 'Matteo, I thought you could do better than that for me. I want a very exclusive party. Perhaps I need to organise it for myself.'

'I will sort it,' Matteo said. 'Do you want to go home first?'

'Yes, then we will go straight from there to the hotel. It has been a long wait….' He told Matteo to slow down and he halted the car and the window slid open and Malvolio called over Pino, a young boy who cycled around town, delivering messages.

'Hey, Pino…' Malvolio said but, instead of giving his instructions in front of Matteo, got out to speak to the young boy and then returned to the car.

'Now it will be a good night,' Malvolio said.

They drove on to Malvolio's home and Angela, his housekeeper, greeted him anxiously.

Malvolio took a drink of whisky and so too did Matteo. Then Matteo paced the floor, making calls to the hotel to arrange the party as the fat man showered and changed and then came down in a loud suit.

Malvolio was, Matteo noted, still sweating even after a shower.

He was repulsive.

'You look nervous,' Malvolio commented when he saw Matteo's strained features. Usually Matteo was the coolest of the lot.

'Why would I be nervous?' he asked. In fact, he was asking himself the same thing.

He neither knew nor cared anything about Bella Gatti.

Then he remembered how she blushed around him and a day a couple of years ago when Dino's mouth had gone too far and he had stepped in.

Yes, he noticed her more than he cared to admit to and he could not stand what awaited her tonight, but for now all attention had to be placed on Malvolio, who was grilling him.

'I thought you would be honoured to find out that you are to be my second man.'

And Matteo knew his life depended on his response.

'Now that you have said that I shall be...' Matteo smiled '...I don't need to be nervous. I'm honoured, Malvolio. I thought Luka would be your choice.'

'Your friend thinks about sex but will soon be grovelling. For now he tries to make up with Sophie.' He looked at Matteo. 'Sophie is too much like her mother, Rosa.' He made a yapping motion with his hands. 'She talks too much, and says no, instead of minding her own business. Luka will soon tire of her. Anyway...' Malvolio shrugged '...we all know what happened to Rosa.'

Matteo took a belt of his drink before he spoke. 'I have to admit that I was worried, if not Luka, that you might consider Dino,' he said, referring to his brother.

'Dino talks too much, everyone knows what is going on in that stupid head of his because he tells them, whereas you...' He looked at Matteo and still he could not read him. That Matteo cared about no one was either a blessing or a curse. It would prove a blessing if he stayed loyal and a curse if he ever again attempted to stray. For now Malvolio chose to practise what he was about to preach. 'Tonight,' Malvolio said, 'is not a night for questions. Tonight is all about putting people at ease. A lot of my men were forced to give evidence. They had to say things about me that they did not want to...'

Matteo nodded.

'Tonight you are to let them know, as I shall, that I understand the pressure they were under. You are to tell them that there are no bad feelings, that I understand that they did what they had to do.'

Matteo let out a small breath of relief, but it did not go far, it halted even before it had fogged the glass as Malvolio spoke on.

'Tonight let them think they are forgiven. Tomorrow you make sure that they pay. All of them.'

He meant Luka also, Matteo knew. Malvolio would even make an example of his own son.

Thank God that Luka was getting the hell out.

Matteo drove them to the hotel. It was starting to get dark and as they came down the hill the sun was firing the ocean so that it rippled like molten lava. As he parked the car and they walked into the hotel, Matteo felt as if he were entering the gates of hell.

CHAPTER SEVEN

As the convoy that would take Paulo Durante to a prison in Rome left, Bella took Sophie back to her home as the photographers packed up.

'It's just news to them,' Sophie said. 'This is my father's life.'

'Come on,' Bella said, and they walked up the hill.

Since the arrests Sophie had lived with Bella and her mother as Malvolio had had his lawyer take ownership of Paulo's home to cover legal fees.

Sophie wasn't upset yet—instead, she was furious. Her father had taken the fall for the entire town's dark dealings. Aside from that, months of pent-up frustration and the pain of hearing Luka say on the stand that he considered her a peasant all flooded out now.

'He humiliated me,' Sophie choked. 'I bet right now he is with his father, toasting their freedom.'

'You know that he's not,' Bella said.

'He said, under oath, that I threw myself at him, even after he had dumped me.'

'He said that rather than admit, in court, that you and he were making plans to leave together,' Bella reminded her friend as they walked. 'You told Luka that you were worried about the things your father was getting up to. How would you feel now if that was the reason your father was being locked away?'

'Well, it did no good,' Sophie hissed. 'Because he *has* been locked away. Luka called me a peasant to his father…'

That would have hurt, Bella knew.

Luka had spent the last few years in London and Bella knew Sophie had felt left behind and not good enough.

Having Luka, however reluctantly, confirm that in court had been cruel to hear indeed. 'Luka cares about you. Remember that he was trying to get away from his father when it all happened and he said those things.' Over and over Bella had told her Luca hadn't meant what he'd said, that he had only been trying to protect Paulo, but this evening Sophie didn't want to hear it.

'I'm going to Rome to be near my father and you need to leave too,' Sophie urged. 'Malvolio is back and all his yes-men are still here.'

'I cannot leave my mother,' Bella said.

'She will understand…'

'I can't, Sophie, she is so sick.' Bella wanted to leave, more than anything she wanted to run, but she knew she could not leave her mother.

They stepped into Bella's small home. Sylvia, her mother's friend, had dropped in to see Maria and bring her up to date with all that had happened. She had bought her some flowers and a bottle of *limoncello* to cheer her up on this very dark day.

Bella waved and called hello and then went into the bedroom the friends were now sharing. Sophie immediately started packing, still urging Bella to come with her, but when a knock came at the door Bella was quite sure, as she went to answer it, that it was Luka, wanting to finally, after all these months, speak with Sophie.

Hopefully he would have better luck calming her down than she'd had, Bella thought.

Only, instead of Luka, when she opened the door she saw young Pino, balancing on his bike and telling her that he had a message from Malvolio. Bella stood there in silence as her fate was delivered—she was to be at the bar tonight.

Bella had always known this day was coming.

It had been as inevitable as breathing if your name was Gatti. A direct assumption that Malvolio had made long ago.

A few months ago Gina had dropped off a package, telling her that on the night of Sophie and Luka's engagement Malvolio had said he wanted her to stay back and to start working at the bar.

The package still lay in her wardrobe unopened.

A reprieve had been granted to Bella in the shape of the arrests but it would seem that her stay of execution was over now.

Bella had, as the trial had neared its end, silently dreaded just this.

She had gone on the Pill just in case and every night when she took it, she told herself that it was unnecessary, that soon, once Malvolio had been put away, she'd be laughing to herself at the fear she had held inside these past months.

Bella closed the door on Pino and went back into the bedroom.

'No,' Sophie said as Bella returned. 'You can tell Luka that I don't want to see him.'

'It wasn't Luka. It was Pino with a message for me.'

Sophie looked up from her case when she heard the tremor in Bella's voice.

'There is to be a big celebration tonight at the hotel, everyone is to be there and I am to work in the bar.'

'No!' Sophie was even more insistent that Bella join her in Rome but Bella shook her head.

'I know that you have to leave and not just to take care of Paulo—you are the scapegoat now. Everyone knows it is Malvolio but that is not what they will say to his face.' Bella started to cry. 'I don't want my first to be Malvolio. I know that you think I should just say no to him.'

'I know that it is not that simple.' Sophie put her arm around her friend and Bella took a cleansing breath.

'She's too ill to even leave the house now,' Bella said about her mother.

'I know.'

'She can't work. Malvolio made her sign over the house, promising to take care of her medical bills… now she owes him rent. How can I leave her to deal with it all? How can I let my mother face his temper if I leave?'

She couldn't.

They both knew that Bella never would.

'When my mother has gone, and it won't be long, then I will come to Rome and be with you, but not now. I need to be here for her in the same way that you need to be there for your father.'

She was grateful that Sophie did not try to dissuade her further and this time, when there was a knock at the door, it *was* Luka and after a few moments of indecision Sophie agreed that she would go for a walk with him.

'Will you wait for me to get back?' Sophie asked, but Bella shook her head.

'I have to be at the bar soon.'

'But I'm flying tonight. I don't know when I'll see you again…'

'It is better that we just say goodbye now,' Bella said. She just wanted it over and done with, before she gave in and broke down.

They stood in the hall and embraced as Luka waited outside.

'We're sisters,' Sophie said, 'maybe not in blood…'

'Sisters in shame,' Bella said, because after tonight that was how she would be. 'But at least try and listen to what Luka has to say when you speak with each other. Don't lose him now, Sophie.'

'He lost me when he said what he did,' Sophie said, and after one final cuddle she walked out.

As Bella walked back down the hall her mother was still chatting to her friend so Bella went into her bedroom, opened the wardrobe and took out the package Gina had dropped off all those months ago.

Inside there was a cheap, black satin dress along with black underwear and sheer stockings. There was make-up and a bottle of perfume too, and Bella sprayed it, screwing up her nose at the cheap, musky scent. There were high-heeled, black strappy sandals and Bella slipped off one of her flat pumps and tried the sandal on.

It was far too small.

But she was no Cinderella and there would be no prince tonight and so, with her mother still talking with her friend, Bella crept into Maria's bedroom.

She went into her mother's wardrobe and, sure enough, there were several pairs of similar sandals to choose from. Bella gave a pale smile as she pulled a pair out. The rubber stopper came off and revealed hollow heels, and as she picked them up and made to go out she glanced up at the chest of drawers and saw the picture of her father and a much younger, far happier and infinitely more beautiful Maria.

Bella knew little about her father. Her mother had never told her very much—just that his name had been Pierre, he'd been French and had been a rich businessman.

Bella paused for a moment and looked at the photo. He had straight black hair and Bella had inherited her pale skin and green eyes from him too.

Hearing her mother's friend say that she should get going, Bella quickly came out of her mother's room and hid the shoes, before heading back out to the kitchen where her mother now sat alone.

'Are you wearing perfume?' Maria asked, screwing up her nose.

'No,' Bella said, and then remembered the scent she had sprayed in the bedroom that must have clung to her. 'Sophie put some on, she has gone for a walk with Luka.'

'What did Pino want?' Maria had more questions. 'I heard him come to the door.'

'He just asked if we would be at the celebrations tonight,' Bella answered nonchalantly.

'And what did you say?'

'I said that you were too tired and that I was already working.' She saw Maria's eyes narrow. 'I have an extra shift doing the turn-down service. There are a lot of extra guests tonight at the hotel now that Malvolio has been released.'

'It's a sad day for Bordo Del Cielo,' Maria said.

'It is,' Bella admitted. Her voice was more husky than usual as she tried to form normal words. 'Sophie is going to Rome to be closer to Paulo.'

'Sophie should live her own life,' Maria said.

'Perhaps.' Bella shrugged.

'I think I might have an early night.' Maria went to stand and Bella put her arm around her waist and walked with her to her bedroom. 'I'll call you if I need you in the night.'

'I've told you,' Bella said. 'I'm working tonight.'

'You'll be home by ten, though,' Maria checked, and Bella nodded, but her heart hurt at the thought of her mother calling out for her in the night and her not being there to answer.

'I love you, Ma.'

'I know that you do.'

With her mother in bed Bella started to get ready. The underwear felt scratchy and her hands were shaking as she pulled on the lacy stockings and clipped the suspenders on.

She set to work with the make-up and put on eyeliner and loads of mascara and rouged her cheeks and then painted her lips a deep red. Her hair she backcombed and then tied into a loose, high bun and sprayed it in place.

Very deliberately, Bella didn't cry.

Not because she didn't want to ruin her make-up—
she was scared that if she broke down she might not stop.

Bella slipped on the cheap black satin dress but she
knew the high heels would make too much noise on
the floor and that her mother might hear so she decided to carry them until she was outside. Dressed like
hell and feeling the same, she went into the kitchen
and put the flowers her mother's friend had left into a
vase. She picked up the *limoncello* and tipped it down
the sink in case her mother was tempted to drink it in
the night. Then, trying to deny her own terror, holding
her shoes in her hand and with her bag on her shoulder, Bella crept through the house.

'Bella!' Her mother called her name from the bedroom. Bella, who was at the front door, froze for a
moment.

'Bella, I need to speak to you.'

'I can't now, Ma,' she called. 'My shift starts soon.'

'Please, Bella, it will just take a moment.'

'I really do have to go.' Bella wrenched open the
door but her mother's voice, though lately so weak,
was suddenly strong.

'You will get back in this house now and come into
my room.'

She quietly closed the door and turned and walked
back along the small corridor. She opened the bedroom door and saw that her mother's side light was on.
Bella would wish for ever that it hadn't been, because
she would always remember the agony on her mother's
features when she saw how her daughter was dressed,
and she would be able to recall, with complete clarity,
the sob of anguish that Maria made.

'Please, no, Bella. You're better than that. You don't

have to do this! Go with Sophie to Rome. I've heard you both talking. Please get away from here, rather than do this. I'm begging you to.'

It would be the easiest thing in the world to go with her friend tonight, to run to put her past behind her, but Bella knew it was impossible.

She knew Malvolio would take out his temper on her terribly frail mother, knew only too well the price her mother would pay—and she had paid enough in her time.

'I'm not leaving you, Mum.'

'I'm asking you to.'

'Never.' Bella shook her head and sat down on the bed. 'I could never leave you behind.'

And she couldn't afford to take her mother with her.

Even if she could somehow find the money for the flights, what would happen when they got to Rome? She and Sophie might be able to live rough for a few days or weeks till they found a job but her mother could not live on the streets.

'Listen to me for five minutes,' Maria said, as Bella stood to go. 'I'm going to tell you something. I've had it tough but I've had some good times. Most of my clients were cruel, hard work but some I considered lovers. I know men, Bella. They moaned to me that they wished their wives would do things that I did, that they were more like me, yet for all their talk they would never take me as their wife. I can't stop you, but I can tell you that everything will change if you go to work tonight. It's a stigma that you can never escape from.' And then Maria told her some information that had always been missing when Bella had tried to piece together her life.

'Your father,' Maria said, and she gestured to the photo. 'I met him when I had just turned sixteen. Long before the hotel had been built there were a few cafés that lined the beach. You know that he was from France and a rich businessman?'

Bella nodded. She wasn't sure she believed her mother but she listened to what she had to say. 'He was here because he was looking into the possibility of putting a hotel here. It was going to be beautiful. Pierre wanted to keep the houses and cafés and blend it in with the mountain. Sicily was a tourist destination but not in the west. We are a bit of a mystery. But that was why he kept coming back, although I like to think he came back in part for me. I thought we were in love and looking back I think that we were.

'Malvolio soon caught on that Pierre had plans for this place and saw to it that he left. I found out that I was pregnant after he had gone back to France. It caused a huge scandal. My parents were furious and devastated but I was sure Pierre would do the right thing.

'I wrote to him as I didn't have his phone number but I knew his business name and I told him that I was pregnant. It was then that I found out that he was married. I can't tell you how much that hurt, Bella. I had always thought that the only thing keeping us apart was distance. I had hoped that when the hotel was built he would live here instead...'

Bella looked at the tears on her mother's cheeks. She had never seen Maria cry, she was the strongest woman Bella knew.

'Did he dump you?' Bella asked.

'Worse than that, or at least I thought so at the

time—he suggested that I come back to France with him. He had no intention of leaving his wife but said that I could be his mistress. I'd have my own apartment and he would visit us when he could. Do you know what I said? I told him that I would never be a kept woman.' Maria let out a hollow laugh at the irony of it all. 'I told him I would never share a man and that it was her or me. He chose her and then I had you, Bella. You were the best thing that ever happened in my life but I couldn't support you. My parents would have nothing to do with me and I was sleeping on the floor at Gina's. Malvolio would often visit her and suggested that I could earn some money... I'm sure you can guess the rest,' Maria said, and Bella nodded.

'You haven't guessed it, though,' Maria said, and Bella frowned. 'I had been working a few months for Malvolio when Pierre came back. He had left his wife and had decided that he was going to come and live here and build the hotel. Malvolio didn't own everything back then and Pierre had it pretty much worked out. We would be together, he said, but then he found out how I had survived that year without him. Bella, I'll never forget the look on his face, he was completely disgusted.'

'He was cheating...'

'Different standards,' Maria said. 'I lost the love of my life and I don't want the same thing happening to you.'

'I understand, but I don't have a lover to lose,' Bella said.

'You will one day and when you do, how will you tell him about your past?'

Bella didn't answer, she simply couldn't think that far ahead.

'And what about Matteo Santini? You've had a thing for him for ages.'

'There's nothing between us. I have liked him for a long time, yes, but word has it that he is now Malvolio's second in charge. He's busy arranging Malvolio's party tonight. I thought he was different but I guess I was wrong about him—he's just as bad as Malvolio or he will be soon.'

'You don't know that,' Maria said. 'I remember his father. He was a kind man and then when he died and that brute moved in…' Maria shook her head as she recalled those times. 'I was only young but I can still remember everyone talking about how he made Matteo's life hell. Matteo started going around to Luka's—he got food there, I guess, and time with his friend, but he paid the price with his friend's father. I've told you what Matteo did for Talia?'

'Many times.' Bella smiled because her mother knew all the town secrets.

'Get out while you can, Bella.'

'I shall get out *when* I can,' Bella said, and she was honest. 'I'm here for as long as you are and then I'm done.'

'Promise me that much,' Maria said.

'I do. One day I'll be in Rome with Sophie and all of this I'll leave behind, but I really do have to go now,' she said.

She didn't want to sit and dwell on Matteo and neither did she want to hear any more about her father who had left them both to this fate.

She gave her mother a kiss, and, not having to

worry about being heard now, she strapped on her high sandals and then headed out into the night, painted and ready to do what she had to do.

CHAPTER EIGHT

THE FOYER HAD been rapidly dressed with pungent flowers and their scent was so sweet and sickly that it reminded Matteo of impending death.

He walked into the bar, to cheers, handshakes and backslaps, and they were not just for Malvolio but also for his new prodigy.

'Tonight we drink, we eat and then we…' Malvolio said. 'I see that Pino has delivered my message.'

Matteo glanced over to where Malvolio was looking and his rapidly beating heart was suddenly still.

Bella was dressed in a small black dress, her tiny bust was jacked up and she had a lot of make-up on. Her thick black hair had been teased and was worn up and he could see her shaking hands as she over-filled a glass.

As she went to get a cloth to mop up her mess she caught his eye and he saw the fear there, but she pushed out a professional smile.

She was working for the first time tonight, Matteo realised, and he looked over at Malvolio and saw his leer.

Gina said something to her and Bella filled two glasses and then handed them both a drink. Instead of taking a seat at his usual table, which was waiting for the guest of honour, Malvolio went behind the bar and checked the CCTV cameras that were in the elevators. They also ran the length of the hotel corridors and out to the foyer and pool, and as he flicked through them he asked for the books to be brought to him.

'I thought we partied tonight,' Matteo said.

'We shall, but first I want to see how well you have taken care of things.' Malvolio frowned as he saw that the staff now kept their tips.

'They work harder,' Matteo said.

'They don't need money to work harder,' Malvolio said. 'You are too soft with them.'

'Look at the return guests,' Matteo said. 'Look at—'

'You think you do better than me?'

Bella glanced over—she could hear the warning in Malvolio's voice. He would loathe it that Matteo had done better at running the hotel than him. Malvolio would detest it that the hotel was thriving without his stranglehold on the place.

'I don't see your girlfriend here tonight.' Malvolio looked around at the bar.

'Tina and I broke up,' Matteo said. Tina had been a vague constant, an excuse Matteo had kept up so that he could go home at night and a reason he could use not to attend Malvolio's more twisted parties.

With Malvolio safely behind bars, Matteo had ended things.

'Good,' Malvolio said. 'Tonight, finally we might see Matteo party.' He snapped his fingers and Bella brought over some more drinks and Matteo knew that he had better think fast.

'I always wanted Bella,' Matteo said, as she walked off, and he knew she must have heard because he watched her falter for a brief second and her already tense shoulders pull back a touch.

Malvolio just laughed. 'Tough.'

They took their seats and sambuca was brought over. Gina served the drinks.

'I missed you, Malvolio,' she lied. 'It's good to have you back.'

Tonight she joined the whole of Bordo Del Cielo in lying just to survive.

Bella felt sick. She had since the verdict had come in but now, since Malvolio had walked in, she felt dizzy with fear.

For close to a year she had dreaded this night. With Malvolio's arrest she had been brought a reprieve but that had run out.

That he was here with Matteo, his new right-hand man, hurt terribly too. Her heart ached as to how the man she had adored from afar was turning out.

Always dark and brooding, some said that Matteo had no emotion. Some said he had been born bad, just like his brother.

Bella had thought she'd known different.

She had adored him but on hearing his lewd comment about her to Malvolio she had actually fought with herself not to turn around and give him a sharp-mouthed response.

She glanced over as Malvolio said something and Matteo did not laugh or smile. Instead, he stood up and walked back in her direction and came over to the bar.

'See that the drinks keep coming.'

'Of course.'

'Mine is at midday,' Matteo said, and Bella frowned and looked down at the tray as he picked up the drink that was on it and then downed it in one.

'I want to keep a clear head,' Matteo said as she went to refill it, and he gestured his head towards the iced water. Bella nodded her understanding—she would give him water from now on.

'Bella…' he said, and he didn't continue. He just gave her a look, a long slow look that Bella didn't understand.

Matteo couldn't tell her his thoughts and what he was planning but with his eyes he implored her to listen to him, to somehow know that he was on her side.

She gave a rapid blink she was confused by the looks she was getting tonight and then looked away.

It was the first time she had heard him say her name.

It killed that it was tonight.

The bar noise grew louder.

Bella, who had never set foot inside one, loathed it. The noise jarred her already shot nerves, the looks from the men she served made her feel ill, but hardest of all were the constant reminders from Gina to smile.

'At least look as if you're enjoying yourself,' Gina said.

'Why?' Bella retorted. 'Do you think any of them care if I am?'

'Lose the smart mouth, Bella,' Gina warned. 'Take them over another tray of drinks and tell them that the food is on its way. Given how he was starved in prison, strange he didn't lose any weight,' Gina scoffed, and even Bella managed a small laugh.

She poured the tray of drinks and took them over. Matteo took the prearranged drink but as soon as he replaced his glass Malvolio handed him another.

'Here,' said Malvolio, and without missing a beat Matteo took it.

Malvolio was testing him, Bella was sure.

'Suddenly I'm hungry,' Malvolio said, with his eyes on Bella as she bent over to retrieve the tray.

'And me,' Matteo said, and Bella froze as his hand slid over her bottom.

Please let it be an accident, she thought, but his hand did not lift and she felt his fingers dig in.

Her instinct was to turn and slap him. She had been as prepared as she could be to take it from Malvolio but to have Matteo treat her like this had temper rather than repulsion building in her.

'No, no,' Malvolio said. 'She's for me, aren't you, Bella?'

She pushed out that smile. 'I hope so...'

'So where are the perks?' Matteo asked, and not just his words had Bella's heart sink but the feel of his hand now running up the inside of her skirt. She closed her eyes but his hand went no higher than the top of her stocking, just hovered at the lace on her thigh.

Malvolio looked at Matteo, the one man who had dared to tell him he expected perks and be treated better than the rest.

Gina placed a huge plate of food in front of him— shrimp, fried cheese, steak and chicken wings.

'You know what I like,' Malvolio said, licking his lips, and then he looked from Gina to Bella.

He could not be bothered with drama and fear tonight, he was tired, he wanted the familiar, not that he would ever admit it.

'Take her now,' Malvolio said to Matteo. 'Now, before I change my mind…' He picked up his fork and Matteo removed his hand from up Bella's skirt and stood.

Not Matteo, she silently pleaded as he took her arm. Not like this.

He was leading her out of the bar, towards the back exit and the stinking alley, and then she heard Malvolio call to him. 'Where are you going?'

'Out the back…' Matteo said.

'You are my second man.' He snapped his fingers to Gina and she nodded for them to come to her and she handed Matteo a room card.

'No.' It was the first time Bella had said it but it fell on deaf ears. Without a word Matteo led her out of the bar and through the foyer and into the elevator.

'Matteo, no…'

It was like the worst nightmare colliding with the best dream; it was worse than anything she had imagined, because it was a man she had cared about who was treating her like this.

'Bella, just go with it,' Matteo said. 'I'll explain soon. You're going to have to trust me for now.'

'Never.'

Malvolio came to the bar and watched the CCTV and saw Bella dragging her feet, and at one point she broke free and ran…

'Bella!' Matteo grabbed her and she fought him.

She swore at him.

Matteo knew, he was positive, in fact, that they were being watched, and so he laughed and sneered at her.

He kissed her hard against the wall, he muffled her cries and ran his hand again over her skirt, and she fought him but there was no chance against his strength.

He dragged her down the hall and into the elevators and Bella went to bite him in the hope of running again, but Matteo slapped her cheek.

It was a stinging slap, a hard slap that left her shocked and stunned that he could ever do this. Not just to her. That the man she had held a torch for could turn into a monster before her eyes. He was nothing like she had imagined.

Tears rose in her eyes and she let out a silent sob as they spilled out. Not that he cared, his rough kisses took her all the way up to the top floor.

'Good boy,' Malvolio said, and then headed back to his steak and shrimp. 'You know, I always thought he was a bit soft. It would seem that I had him wrong.'

Bella, as Matteo pushed her into the hotel room, was thinking exactly the same.

CHAPTER NINE

'IT'S OKAY…'

She was still fighting him but he pulled her right into him the moment the door closed on them, just so she wouldn't run.

'We're alone now.'

His words did not soothe Bella.

She had dreamt of being alone with Matteo, only it had never, ever been anything like this.

Her cheek was stinging from his slap, her arm was sore where he had grabbed her roughly, and now he was trying to calm her.

'I thought better of you…!' Bella shouted, trying to push him off.

'We're not going to do anything,' Matteo said. 'I knew that Malvolio would be watching on the cameras so I had to be rough, but I'm telling you now that I'm not going to hurt you, Bella, I'm not going to touch you.'

He was rough for the last time with her. He practically peeled a raging Bella off him and pushed her onto the bed, where she sat for a long moment.

Her breathing was starting to slow down, his words were filtering in and starting to make sense. She knew that there were cameras in all of the corridors—Malvolio watched his staff like a hawk—but here in the hotel rooms there were none.

The long look that Matteo had given her downstairs was starting to make sense, along with the restraint in his fingers. He had been trying to get her away from Malvolio.

'You could have told me.'

'I tried to.'

'You could have tried harder,' she hurled at him—her heart was still beating too fast and her veins pumped with adrenaline. 'You should have explained.'

'What, and walk up to the suite holding hands?' Matteo scorned. 'I'm sorry I hit you, that it came to that, but had you run back down there…'

Bella nodded, she got it now.

She looked at the surroundings. At the time she had paid no attention to where Matteo had been taking her but, from working here, she knew the room.

'I guess Malvolio gets the presidential suite?' Bella said.

It was a cheap hotel but, still, it was far more luxury than she was used to.

The French windows were open but it was a hot and sultry night and there was only the occasional breeze. The ceiling fan above the bed was turned off and she glanced up at it.

'Do you want it on?' he asked.

'Isn't it supposed to be about what you want?' Bella asked, as he flicked the switch and the fan whirred into life, but Matteo just went back to resting against the wall.

'So we just wait here?' Bella asked.

'Yes.'

He expected her to be relieved, for thanks even, but instead his eyes narrowed as she gave a mocking laugh.

'Oh, Matteo the big saviour,' Bella said. 'Don't you see that all you've done is delay the inevitable? How can that possibly help me?'

'You don't have to…' He stopped. In this town, all too often, there was no choice. 'You could leave tonight.'

She didn't deign a response but he pushed on.

'I hear that Sophie is following her father to Rome. You could go with her tonight. I might have fallen asleep after sex…'

'So I can be homeless and poor in Rome.'

'Not for long,' Matteo said. 'You would find your feet, I am sure.'

'Thanks but, no thanks, for the reprieve,' she said, and he went and sat in a chair as she got up from the bed and roamed the room.

She saw a bottle of wine and picked it up.

'Open it,' Matteo said.

'I thought you said that you wanted a clear head.'

'It's the last thing I want now.' He felt ill seeing the mark on her cheek. Her cheap dress was torn and the fear he had heard in her voice had Matteo's heart still pounding.

Not that he showed it.

She poured two glasses, though with far steadier hands than she had downstairs, and as she passed one to him their fingers met, and so did their eyes. Bella gave him a small nod, perhaps of thanks, because she knew he had only been trying to help.

There was no help to be had, though.

She wandered out to the balcony and stood there, gazing at the darkening night, and after a few moments he joined her. She turned just a little and gave him a pale smile before returning to the view she loved so. 'Africa is less than a hundred miles away...' Bella said. 'Right there...' she pointed into the darkness, knowing the exact direction '...is Kelibia. I used to practise swimming, thinking I could escape to there if I had to.'

'You can,' Matteo said. 'Well, you couldn't swim to Kelibia but everyone is in the bar, people think you are here, and so you *could* leave tonight, and be in Rome by morning.'

'I can't leave my mother,' Bella said, and then she rephrased it because she had had offers to do just that tonight. 'I don't *want* to leave my mother,' she corrected.

'You'd rather this life?'

'Nobody *wants* this type of life,' she said, and then threw him a look. 'What would you know? You're one of them.'

Matteo never gave away what he was thinking, he never really said much at all unless he had to. He saw her place the wine glass on her burning cheek to cool it and, no, he would not tell her that he knew plenty. Neither would he reveal that he had a one-way ticket out of hell in the morning. But tonight he decided to tell her a little of his past instead, in the hope it might make her leave. 'I do know, though.'

She turned and looked at him.

'I tried to leave once,' Matteo admitted. 'It was a couple of years ago—the night of the Natalia street party—and I hoped Malvolio would be too busy to notice I had gone until it was too late…'

'I remember that night,' Bella said, though she did not tell him yet just why she remembered it.

'Earlier in the week I had told my brother that I'd had enough and that I was getting out.'

'What did Dino say?'

'Not much. Well, not much to me. He said plenty to Malvolio, though.' Matteo was quiet for a long time before he spoke again. 'There's one road out of this place, Bella, and I used it. I got out of town and I made it to just past the river. I tried to hitchhike as I walked but no one stopped until…'

'Malvolio?'

Matteo nodded, and, just as on that night, his face did not betray the fear that had gripped him as he'd watched that large red car pull up beside him. How, as Malvolio had opened his window to speak with him, he had glimpsed the gun beneath his jacket and Matteo had thought he would be left dead in the street.

'What did he do?'

'He told me to get in and we went for a drive.' Every moment of that drive he had known that it might well be his last. 'He took me to dinner—you know how he likes to pretend he is a reasonable man?'

Bella nodded.

'I can think on my feet faster than anyone, Bella. I knew that if I told him the truth, I was finished. I knew that if I started grovelling and apologising then I'd be done for so, instead of showing him my fear, I showed him my anger…'

Bella frowned. She couldn't imagine him scared, yet he had just admitted to fear, and neither could she imagine anyone getting angry with Malvolio and getting away with it.

'I told him I was sick of being treated the same as all the others. I told him I was older than Dino, smarter than Dino and that I was more loyal to him than all the rest. I said that I wanted more respect, I wanted to be paid more than the others and to look smarter than the rest.'

'He bought it?'

'In part,' Matteo said. 'Now he gets some tailor from Milan over once a year and that is why Malvolio dresses like a golf player and that is why I look like a soccer star out on the pull.'

She laughed and he realised he was smiling as she did so.

'I like how you dress,' Bella said. 'But, then, I love fashion.'

She looked at his smile and the shiver that ran down her arms wasn't from fear or the slight cool breeze, it was that she was alone with him and his deep voice was beautiful.

'He doesn't fully trust me, though,' Matteo admitted, and then he looked at Bella. 'With reason.'

'Why are you telling me this?'

'I'm telling you because I do know how hard it is to get out of this place. There are few chances to do so—the night of the Natalia party I hoped was mine, but this night could be yours.'

'That night, at the party, I was waiting for you...'

'Why?'

'I've liked you for a long time,' Bella admitted, and she watched a small frown line form between his eyes. Matteo was used to women liking him but it was the way she admitted it so openly, so honestly that had him a touch taken back. 'Didn't you already know that?' she asked.

'No.'

'You think my cheeks are always this pink?' Bella laughed. 'Then you must also assume that I have a stammer.'

'I've never…' He was about to say that he had never given her that much thought but then he found himself smiling again as he nodded. 'Yes, I did notice you blush and mess up your words but I just thought you were very shy…'

'No, I'm not in the least shy,' she said. 'I just get a little tongue-tied whenever you are around.'

'Well, you're certainly not tongue-tied now.'

She wasn't, she realised. Perhaps because she was speaking now with the man she had always somehow known he was.

'I'm still blushing, though.'

Her small provocation was unexpected, both welcome and unwelcome. Welcome to his body but not to his head, for he had brought her up here so that she could avoid all that.

'You don't have to do that, Bella.'

'Do what?'

'Play the game.'

It just didn't feel as if she was.

As the phone in the room started ringing Bella gave a wry, hollow laugh.

'They'll be wanting to know why you're not back down there—you should be finished with me by now.'

Matteo went in to answer and as he picked up the phone Bella closed her eyes when he told Gina that he was here for the night and to pass on the message to Malvolio. What he said was crude but it clearly appeased Malvolio because from the open French windows she heard the cheer go up from the bar below as undoubtedly the message was relayed.

'Come inside,' Matteo said.

'Why?' she asked. 'So that we can eat the free nuts and drink the cheap wine? It doesn't change the outcome, Matteo. You only delay the inevitable. Don't you get it that you're not saving me here? I'm not Talia with my children all gathered up by the back door and ready to get out.'

'How do you know about that?' Matteo frowned. 'Talia would never tell anyone.'

'Except perhaps her husband,' Bella said, and then she smiled at Matteo's frown. 'My mother knows everyone's business. Men tell her things that they would not dare speak of when they are in the bar.' The smile slid from her face then. 'Tomorrow night I'll be back working, and guess what? It's going to hurt a whole lot more than it would have with you.'

'Don't talk like that.'

'Why not?' she said. 'It's the truth.' He opened his mouth to argue but she spoke over him. 'Please, don't suggest again that I leave. If you want to help me then…'

'Then what?'

Bella stared out at the dark Mediterranean, to the escape route that she had always deep down known was an impossible one but at least it had kept hope alive. Tonight, though, she could have a part of that dream. Tonight, even if it was just a little while, one of her wishes could come true.

'You could make love to me. I don't want my first time to be rough…' she said, and he closed his eyes and shook his head but she persisted. 'I know what my future is going to be but I would like it to be different for my first time.'

'You want me to break you in for others?' Matteo sneered.

'Yes,' she said. 'But I also want you to show me how good it could be.'

'Should be.'

'Not for the likes of me,' she said, and she was not playing the martyr, she just knew how it was. 'Are you a considerate lover, then?' She smiled and so did Matteo, because his own 'should be' response had caught him by surprise.

'No.'

'It's really not my lucky night, then, is it?' Bella shrugged.

Why, he wondered, did she make him smile? There was something about her openness, born perhaps from colourful discussions with her mother, yet the tease to her voice was still somehow sweet.

'Hey,' Bella said, 'maybe I could be like Gina—available just for you.'

Matteo looked at her with his near-black eyes and he was on the edge of telling her the truth—that in the morning he would be gone.

It was too dangerous to do that, though.

He didn't really know Bella at all.

'That's not going to happen,' he said instead.

'So we just have tonight?' she checked, and he nodded. 'We could rewrite history, then.'

'How?'

'Perhaps you did come to the Natalia party after all. We could dance as we might have danced that night…'

'I don't dance,' he said.

'Neither do I.' Bella shrugged but then she put down her glass and walked over and wrapped her arms around his neck, and for Matteo it was his last night on the edge of heaven, with Tunisia but a dream away. Maybe tonight he could dance, could make love, could give her the one night they suddenly both wanted.

'Come inside, then,' he said, and unwrapped her arms from him, and this time they *were* holding hands as they walked into the bedroom.

He closed the French windows behind them and he put on some music to drown out the sounds of the bar below, but he opened the drapes so the moon would later bathe them.

She had dreamt of this moment for ever, the moment that Matteo Santini took her nervous but wanting into his arms.

His fingermarks were still there on her cheek and it was a little bit swollen, and he hated how badly he had scared her. His hand was back on her cheek but gentle now. 'You're going to bruise…'

'It was worth it for him to believe us,' she said.

Malvolio would not believe this, though, she thought as his lips grazed hers.

No one would believe that the brooding, silent man could kiss so gently. The touch of his lips was so feather-light at first that even the scratch of his jaw felt soft to her.

It was, Bella decided, her first kiss because the rough one in the hall and elevator would never count.

He was gentle and tender and there was barely any pressure on her mouth, just the soft caress of his lips, and when he pulled away his lips were as red as hers.

'You're wearing lipstick,' Bella said, and he kissed her again, till their faces were smeared red and their tongues were hot.

The hows and whys that had brought them to this point no longer mattered as they danced their first dance, as they kissed first kisses, as they turned each other on slowly and made believe it was two years ago.

And so it was Christmas, and she pretended that she was sixteen and he *had* come to the street party and wasn't out on the dark streets, looking to escape.

'The street looked beautiful. The trees were all dressed in lights...' She told him about all he had missed. Her voice was a little breathless and her breasts felt as if they had grown for they ached in her tight bra, and he seemed to know that because his hand took the strain of one of them.

'What were you wearing that night?' Matteo asked, as she rested her head on his shoulder and closed her eyes to the soft caress of his hand.

'I had made a dress that was the colour ginger,' Bella said.

'You made it?' he checked.

'I made it with you in mind,' she said. 'You have no idea how beautiful that dress was. I tried make-up for the first time that night and when I went to go out my mother made me wash it off.' She smiled at the memory. 'I told her that that was rich, coming from her.'

'What did she say to that?'

'That if he liked me there would be no need for make-up and perfume.' She moved from his shoulder to meet his gaze. 'Then she asked me what his name was.'

'Did you tell her?'

She nodded.

'And what did she say?'

'To be careful,' Bella admitted. 'Then she told me that perhaps you were not as bad as your brother...' Their hips were swaying, his other hand was feeling her bottom through the dress and she was closer, not just physically but closer and safer than she had ever felt with another person. Oh, Bella loved her mother but Maria's lifestyle meant that Bella had never ever really known how it felt to be truly safe.

Tonight for the first time she did.

She danced and leant on him and then they kissed some more. Her dress was thin and he loathed the padded bra that did not let him stroke her nipples so he slipped the straps of her dress down and she closed her eyes as he removed her bra, sure he would be disappointed.

He wasn't. His thumb caressed her nipple and his palm was warm on her skin as they danced...but as he buried his mouth beneath her hair to kiss her neck he was honest. 'I loathe that scent,' Matteo said.

'So do I.'

'Let's get rid of it, then.'

He ran the bath and then peeled off her dress and they danced in the bathroom for a while longer until the bath was full. Bella, in her underwear and high heels, Matteo still in his suit, and she saw that her make-up had smeared his shirt.

She liked how when he let her go he pulled up his sleeve and put his hand in the water and added more cold water and then he took her hand and she sat on the edge of the bath.

He did not look up as he unclipped her stockings and rolled them down, and she could hear a ragged edge to his breathing as he undid her shoes and undressed her some more.

He kissed the inside of one pale thigh as an apology for his earlier uninvited touch there and Bella's legs were shaking as he kissed the other thigh the same way. She lifted her bottom just enough so that he could take down her panties and suspender belt and he knelt as she sat naked.

The room was warm and steamy and her legs were apart and her throat closed as she silently wished he would kiss her there. Bella knew, though, that if he did she would topple, for even gripping the sides of the bath she was barely steady as his kiss to her thigh deepened.

He could feel her shaking so he stood and took her hand and Bella was helped into a bath for the first time.

She liked it even more as she lay shoulder deep in bubbles and his eyes did not leave her face as he undressed.

'You're getting in?' she asked as she watched him slip off his jacket and hang it behind the door.

'I am,' he said, his eyes never leaving her face. 'I want to be with you rather than simply watching you.'

Bella lay back and she watched as he responded to the slow smile on her face with one of his own.

She had never seen him smile like that. Usually he was ice—his features held closed and his eyes either behind sunglasses or guarded. If he ever did smile, it was usually an arrogant one or a triumphant smirk, but tonight his smile was slow and sensual and for her alone.

He undressed slowly and it was suddenly important to Bella that he did. She had already put out of her mind what had taken place in the corridor but even aside from that, the Matteo she had heard about was neither tender, slow nor patient.

He was tonight.

She watched as he undid the buttons on the front of his shirt and then the sleeves and then he took it off. Bella wanted to reach out and touch his skin. She wanted her fingers on dark, flat nipples as his had been on hers. Soon they would touch but for now she took in the delicious view of his torso. He was masculine and raw in his beauty. Even his arms turned her on as she knew soon they would be wrapped around her and that they would be skin to skin. She watched the stretch of his muscles as he hung his shirt on a hook and her eyes fell on a long, very neat scar.

'What happened?' Bella asked.

'A fight,' he said, and then shook his head. 'I don't want to talk about it.'

He tossed aside his socks and shoes with far less care than his other clothes and she lay there, a dense feeling forming between her legs as he saved the best till last.

He slid open the buckle of his belt.

Too slowly for Bella for, beneath the fabric, she could see his erection bulging.

His tongue he held between his lips as he slid down the zipper.

Bella wasn't even breathing.

The bathroom shrank, steam fogged the mirrors, even her shoulders and face, which were out of the water, were damp.

But her mouth was dry.

She licked her lips as he freed himself and, no, the rest of his clothes he did not hang up, he just stepped out of them.

He was always impressive dressed and yet he was perfection naked.

His calves were lean, his thighs were long and muscular and they would be hers to enjoy later, but all she could focus on now was his erection. Impressive, dark and long, and growing even as she looked, beneath the bubbly water her fists clenched. She lifted her knees as he approached, but not just to make room for him. It was a necessary motion because her thighs ached as they never had before.

He was so tall and had run the bath so deep that the water slipped over the edge as he joined her.

'We don't want to flood the bathroom,' she said, loving the strength of his legs as they moved around the sides of her body and captured her like a vice.

'We might end up crashing through the floor and into the bar,' he said, and he laughed a deep, low laugh, and it was the first time she had heard it.

No one really heard it, Bella was sure, and that made her sad enough for it to show in her expression but he misread it.

'Are you scared?' he asked.

She shook her head. How could she possibly be scared with Matteo gazing into her eyes and his legs holding her body and his hands taking hers in his? Fear had no place here tonight.

He looked at her hands, pale and slender in his, and then he let them go and picked up a cloth when she wanted his kiss. Her lips moved towards him but he moved his head back.

'Patience, Bella.'

'I have none with you.'

'Well, I'm going to teach it to you. Come here, little panda…'

He very carefully started to remove her make-up. The lipstick he had already taken care of with his mouth and she closed her eyes as he removed the streaked eyeliner and mascara and painted her eighteen and innocent again.

He was tender and yet it was so sensually done that her hands could not stay still beneath the water so she explored his thighs, feeling their power and stroking the lean muscle while resisting her true desire to touch him more intimately.

He dipped the cloth in the water again and now, as he removed the last traces of her foundation, her fingers could resist no more—they dusted his thick erection and she watched his jaw clench slightly and her eyes told him it had been no accident.

Her hands then told him the same as she held him more firmly, stroking him between her two hands as he continued on his mission to strip her of her armour.

He soaped her neck with the cloth but he was having trouble concentrating as one of her hands slipped lower and held the weight of his balls as she stroked him closer to the edge.

Her smile was pure decadence and so was his as he pushed her back. Her hands let go of their treasure and he deftly lifted her hips and pulled her towards him so that her hair fell into the water. She floated for a blissful moment as he moved her calves to his shoulders and the view for Matteo was pure temptation.

She came up and rested her arms on the edge of the bath, taking her sex from his immediate view, and he moved her hips further down so she could feel his erection press against her. She nearly died at the lust in his eyes.

Matteo had intended to take things more slowly—to take his time with washing her hair—but now that he'd seen the prettiest of pink it was *his* patience that had run out.

He hauled himself up and climbed out and then lifted her dripping wet body and carried her through to the bed.

He wanted to take her now but he had to taste her first so he knelt down on the floor and dragged her so that her bottom was at the edge of the bed.

Bella lay dizzy. The fan blew air and cooled her damp body and yet her sex was on fire as he parted her thighs and her legs made themselves at home on his shoulders. He splayed her intimate lips with his thumbs and exposed her just a touch more indecently.

Matteo was neither slow nor tender now. He might have teased her with kisses to her thigh, he might have lingered a little longer with his eyes, but a sudden moan of want and frustration from Bella—a sob that gave immediate consent—had Matteo burying his face.

Nothing could have prepared her for the sensations that his mouth delivered. She was wet, not just from the bath, or his tongue, but from her own need.

Her fingers were in his hair, both pressing him in

and pushing him away, and her head thrashed on the damp sheet.

He petted her, he whetted her, he had full sex with her with his mouth.

She would have sat up if she were not falling into the abyss.

Or shout out if her jaws would only open.

When she came, it almost finished him too.

To feel her pulse to his mouth had Matteo reach down to stroke himself, he was so close, but he halted because there was a better pleasure to be had.

Still tasting her, his hand patted the bed, feeling his way to the bedside table where condoms had been so *thoughtfully* placed.

'We don't need them…' Bella gasped, for she had gone on the Pill as a back-up, knowing that this night might arrive.

'You always—'

'We're dating tonight,' she breathed, and it was enough for now, for they were back in the moment, just a couple craving each other.

She moved up the bed and he came over where she lay, still trying to gather her breath.

He kissed her again, his mouth wet from her, his body so hard for her as he butted at her tight entrance. His hand moved down and he held himself, to allow for more precision.

It hurt, even with Matteo trying to be gentle, but as he seared in Bella let out a sob and he gave her a moment and felt her shallow breaths on his cheeks as she attempted to acclimatise.

He held himself there and she thought how the receding pain would lead to bliss.

Then his hand moved away and he drove in fully. Had his weight not come down on her she might have twisted away or pushed him because the hurt was so intense.

He knew she was hurting and so he loved her more slowly. He waited, with patience he had not known that he possessed, until she relaxed a touch around him.

Her thighs loosened, her head cleared and she opened her eyes to his.

She gave a small nod, she sought his lips and thanked him with a kiss, and now when he started to move her fingers, which had dug into his shoulders, loosened their grip and she let him take over and take her to places she had not known existed.

He was incredibly diligent. When she tensed he slowed, when she moaned he persisted, and persisted at the very point where her pleasure seemed to gather towards the most exquisite peak.

Bella tasted his neck and the salt of his shoulder and when still he carried on she could taste no more because her mouth was gasping in air. As she started to come, as her body turned rigid, her breath shallow on his cheek, she was shocked at the intensity of the peak and was just falling into pleasure when he forced her higher. To feel the very controlled Matteo so unleashed and relentless made Bella shout out.

She loved this side to him, the slight roughness, the pursuit of his pleasure, and then the shudder as he shot into her and she came again. She simply slipped into the next falling, holding onto him, tumbling with him so they hit back to earth together, kissing on a soft mattress, lost with each other, having escaped from the world.

Through the night they made love and then both lay there silently dreading the morning, talking to each other, getting to know each other as the moments counted down.

He told her how he wished he'd seen her in the ginger dress she'd made.

'I've still got it,' she said, and she wished, how she wished that he would suggest that soon he see it.

That maybe later, when she wasn't working, he might suggest they go out, that she might wear the same dress for him...

But Matteo said nothing and Bella was starting to understand her mother's words when finally he spoke.

'I bet you would have looked beautiful,' he said.

She belonged in the bedroom now, Bella thought.

She shrugged away the hurt with casual words. 'Cut the cloth right and any figure can be beautiful,' she said. 'I tried to get into some design courses but...' She shook her head. 'Maybe I'm not as good as I think I am.'

'You're probably better,' he said.

'What would you do if you could do anything?'

He was about to find out, Matteo knew. In a few short hours he'd be away from here for ever.

The light was starting to filter in. Morning, whether they were ready or not, was arriving and Matteo climbed out of the bed and opened the French windows.

The party below was over. Bordo Del Cielo lay silent and the only sound was the ocean.

'I love this place,' Bella said. 'I know there are so many bad things that go on here but there is so much beauty too.'

She told him about the ancient baths, which was her favourite place in the world. 'Sometimes I pretend that I was born then, that I lived then, that the baths are still alive.'

'I've never been,' he admitted.

'We could go there,' Bella pushed, trying to pretend that all they had found last night existed, that it didn't end here and now. 'We could take a picnic, just spend the day exploring…'

'A picnic?' His voice was scathing. It was not the sort of thing he would do or had ever done.

'Some wine,' Bella said. 'We could pretend…'

He glanced over but she was staring out at the scenery and his head tightened because he was picturing himself in a place he had never been—exploring with Bella, spending a day doing nothing but being with her.

'Is there any better view?' she asked, but he didn't answer as he headed to the shower.

It wasn't a view to die for, Matteo thought.

Or kill for.

He showered, his intention to dress and go. He didn't know how to leave her, yet there was no way that he could stay.

Matteo wanted to make something of himself. He was sick of the crime and depravity and knew that as of today his role became more serious. He wanted a future, a perfect one, a clean one, to remove himself completely from his past.

Instead of dressing, though, he wrapped a towel around his hips and went into the bedroom, where Bella was still gazing out at the view.

Her hair, which was usually straight, was knotted

and wavy, there a touch of mascara that he must have missed smudged beneath her eyes and her smile was waiting for him.

If ever there was a moment he might regret, this wasn't one of them. It was one Matteo might later question—because instead of dressing and leaving he dropped the towel and got into the bed and took her in his arms and she rested her head on his chest.

It would be his last day here for ever, perhaps—if he returned there would be a bullet waiting with his name on it.

He lay there thinking for a long time and so too did Bella.

All she had wanted was one perfect night and now that she had known one, it made her future somehow worse. She knew she was breaking the deal she had pushed for—one night of making love.

He had given her more than she had asked for and she knew she had to play fair and accept things when he walked away.

Her hand was idly exploring him, stroking his flat stomach and moving the snake of hair in the wrong direction, and the sensation for Matteo must be just right because she could see him hardening and her mouth started to kiss his chest as her hand moved down.

'Bella,' he said finally, 'I have to go soon but first we need to speak.'

'I know that you have to go,' she said. 'But before you do…'

It was her acceptance of him, her lack of demands, that she would kiss him so readily even as he prepared to walk away, that sealed things for Matteo.

He didn't care if it was illogical to feel like this after

only one night. All he knew was that he could no more leave her behind than Bella could leave her mother.

Her mouth moved further down and met with his growing erection.

'Bella,' Matteo said, 'you're coming with me.'

She laughed, her mind not really on the conversation. Certainly she had not known that Matteo had plans to leave and so she corrected the brief miscommunication as she continued her brave kiss, felt his hand move to her head and whispered words that had made him moan.

'No, you're the one who will be coming.'

He tasted soapy and clean and he remained patient. Bella looked up once to find him watching as she took him deeper into her mouth.

Tentatively her tongue explored him, scared of her teeth, that she was doing it wrong, but his fingers tightened in her hair.

'That's it…' he said, when she did not dare go deeper, so she stroked his base with her hand as her tongue continued its exploration.

She remembered how last night he had simply devoured her and growing bolder she started to do the same.

She knelt up and he played with one small breast, delivering gentle twists and pinches as her mouth did the same. The hand on her head exerted just a touch more pressure and yet she resisted and he gave up trying to guide things, to rush things, he just accepted the rare pleasure of an unskilled yet willing mouth.

When he started to come it took him by surprise, and the thrusts and moans from him served as only the briefest of warning. Bella held him alive in her hand, tasting and licking, and that it wasn't enough pressure for him only made his orgasm all the more intense.

'Bella,' he said as she came back to lie by his side, and he was so glad that she did because he could see the confusion in her eyes as he said, 'I'm leaving this morning and you're coming with me.'

'I—'

He didn't wait for her to say that she couldn't; he ended that conflict then and there.

'Your mother too. We're getting out of Bordo Del Cielo.'

CHAPTER TEN

BELLA SAT UNSEEING as the morphine infusion dripped into her mother's thin arm.

Her mind was back on that morning—and all the hope that had carried her home.

That Matteo had said that Maria could come with them had meant everything to her. Not just that it gave her a means to leave but that he had accepted the whole of her heart—the love she had for her mother was a part of Bella.

And, too, he had accepted her mother as a person when all too often Maria's wants and needs and rights to exist safely had been cast aside.

Bella's shoulders and back ached from sitting in a chair all night and long into today but after three months of fighting to live, her mother had finally given in and was fast fading.

A nurse came in and Bella looked up and gave her a tired smile.

'There's a phone call for you, Bella,' she said. 'You can take it in the office…' She gestured to her sleeping mother and Bella was grateful for the nurse's insight because she didn't want to discuss just how ill her mother was beside her bed. 'I'll be in to change your mother's IV soon.'

Bella nodded and stood up. She knew that the next twelve-hour infusion would probably be the last one her mother had. She didn't like to leave her even for a moment but she knew it would probably be Sophie calling—yesterday Paulo had been sentenced.

When she had first arrived in Rome, Sophie had called her friend and Sylvia had been at Bella's home, cleaning up the mess from Maria's fall, and had answered the phone and told Sophie the sad news.

Now Sophie rang when she could, usually from a pay phone, and so of course she wasn't able to speak for long.

'I'm so sorry,' Bella said. 'I saw it on the news.'

'They gave him forty three years minimum,' Sophie said, her voice thick with tears. 'He'll never get out.'

'I know. How is he taking it?'

'He keeps crying, he is very weak and confused, and so worried about me too. I've told him that Luka is here in Rome with me and that he is taking care of me well.'

'Good,' Bella said. 'At least that gives him one less thing to worry about.'

'I have found work,' Sophie said. 'It is at Hotel Fiscella. You have never seen such luxury, Bella…' And then when Bella said nothing Sophie asked the difficult question. 'How is she?'

Bella couldn't speak.

She looked out at the ward and the nurse was going in to change her mother's IV.

'Bella?' her friend pushed gently. 'Tell me.'

'I think she is very near the end.'

Sophie was silent for a long moment too and then she said what she had to to her friend. 'Then you need to make plans.'

'I know,' Bella said. 'After the funeral…'

'Bella, you can't go back there. If you do, he won't let you leave.'

She knew Sophie was right.

Very deliberately Bella had not gone home, telling Malvolio, when he'd dropped in, that her mother drew comfort from her being near.

True.

His patience had just about run out.

'I have to go,' Sophie said. 'I'm using the work phone and I'll get into trouble if I'm caught.'

They said their goodbyes but as Bella stepped into her mother's room she saw that Malvolio had just arrived. He came in every now and then, more, Bella thought, to check on her than Maria.

'The nurse said that you were on the phone.'

'It was a friend…' Bella shrugged '…wanting to see how my mother was.'

'It must be a day for catching up. Matteo called Dino earlier today…'

'That brute,' Bella said, grateful, ever grateful for the bruise Matteo had made on her cheek that night.

Malvolio had been livid that his son and second man had gone and he had grilled Bella over and over about anything Matteo, Luka or Sophie might have told her.

Sophie he cared nothing about, but the leaving of the other two he had taken very personally indeed.

'Matteo asked after you,' Malvolio said, and Bella

shrugged, even though her heart was pounding. She knew that it was important that she did not leap, as she wanted to, at his name. 'Dino didn't tell him about your mother, he didn't know if you might want to keep that private, so instead Dino said that you were enjoying working at the bar...' Malvolio was still determined to find Matteo's Achilles' heel and it took everything Bella had not to react as he spoke on.

'Dino also said how much he was enjoying you.'

She stood silent for a second, willing herself not to react to that vile inference. She could recall Matteo saying that it was important he never reveal that he cared for her and wondered how he would have reacted to Dino's words.

Finally she managed to speak.

'I need to get back to my mother.'

'I hear that she's not doing well at all. She's hung on far longer than we all expected. How long has it been now?' Malvolio asked, and Bella knew what he was implying—Bella had been gone from the bar for far, far too long.

'Three months,' she answered.

'That's a long time to go without work, Bella,' Malvolio said. 'I know you must be worried about funeral costs and things but you don't need to worry, I'll sort that out for you—your mother deserves a dignified send-off.'

Maria's funeral would be Bella's first debt to him.

There was the sudden call of a name and they both turned.

'Bella!'

The nurse who had been sorting out her mother's IV called for her to come quickly and as she stepped into the room Bella understood why, for Maria was taking her last breaths.

Bella cuddled her mother as she left the earth, thanking her for her love and letting her go with grace.

And afterwards she sat by her, knowing in her heart that her mother would understand why she wouldn't be at her funeral.

'If I go back now,' Bella said, 'that will be it.' She knew that much. Malvolio kept his girls too tired to think straight and if they were too tired to work, well, there was always a little something he might slip them to perk them up for that.

'I love you so much,' Bella told her mother, and she gave her one last kiss and took off the little gold and ruby ring her mother wore and slipped it onto her own finger. 'I'll do everything I can to keep it,' she said, though she would sell it if she had to because apart from the clothes she stood up in she had nothing.

The money Matteo had given her had run out—three months living in a chair by her mother's bed, eating from the canteen and buying Maria little luxuries, had taken care of that.

'Bella…' The nurse came in, Bella assumed, to tell her that they were moving Maria now, but instead she had a message for her. 'Your friend asked how much longer you might be.'

'My friend?'

Bella stood as the door opened further and there stood Malvolio. She had assumed he'd gone home, or rather, with her mother dying, she'd simply forgotten that he was there.

'Come on, Bella,' Malvolio said and she saw that Dino stood behind him. 'Let's get you home.'

The nurse had gone but, Bella knew, even if she were here, there would have been little she could do.

The cries she made as Dino walked her down the hospital corridor the staff assumed were for her loss but it wasn't just Maria that Bella mourned.

There was one road out of Bordo Del Cielo and Bella sat silent on the same road back.

Another chance for freedom had gone.

After three months' absence Bella stepped into the home that she had shared with her mother.

Maria's friends had been in and tidied and there were fresh flowers from the garden on the table.

Sicilian funerals were rapid affairs.

That evening a mass was being said for her mother and tomorrow morning she would be buried.

And by tomorrow night Bella would be expected to show up at work.

The only person who might be able to help her was Matteo but she had no idea how to contact him—all she knew was that he had gone to London with Luka.

But then she thought of her mother and how, instead of waiting for Dino to come and collect the rent, she would sometimes call Matteo.

Bella went to the hall table and to her mother's little black book and there, in her mother's handwriting, was his name.

With a shaking hand she called his number but when nothing happened she tried again and then again.

It took a few moments to realise that in her absence the phone had been cut off.

There was a knock at the door and it was one of

her mother's friends, Sylvia, who said she would walk with Bella to mass.

'And I'll be here at seven tomorrow.'

'Seven,' Bella checked.

'It's going to be a busy morning for you, Bella. I'll cook tonight and then we can get the house ready to receive guests.'

Bella thanked her and went into her bedroom to get changed. She wore black and then went into her mother's room to borrow the veil Maria had worn for funerals. She'd had weeks to get used to the idea that her mother was dying but now that she had it felt surreal.

Stepping into her mother's bedroom, Bella could not understand how everything looked the same—her clothes hung in the wardrobe, the photos were out, her silver hairbrush and perfume bottles were all there, and Bella truly felt as if her mother was still with her, as if she might turn and see her lying in the bed.

'Bella,' Sylvia called, 'people are starting to walk over to church.'

The church was full and the wives all greeted her with their lips pursed and their husbands didn't meet Bella's eyes, knowing how many times she had seen them come through her mother's door.

It was a long mass and Bella sat through it, too numb to cry and too scared of tomorrow to mourn her mother yet.

As the congregation spilled out Bella stayed and said more prayers but once back home, instead of cooking for tomorrow, she lay on her mother's bed, with Matteo's phone number in her hand, waiting for darkness. When it came she headed down the street and walked towards the call box.

'Bella?'

She jumped when she heard Malvolio call her name. She had hoped that by now he would be in the bar.

'Where are you off to?'

Think on your feet, Bella. She could almost hear Matteo telling her what to do.

'Just walking…'

'I could walk with you.'

'I was going to go to the church again,' Bella said. 'I want to sit with my mother and say some more prayers for her soul. She will need them…'

Bella saw Malvolio's tense blink.

God still scared him.

And with good reason, Bella thought as he told her that he would pray for Maria's soul too and then walked off.

She spat at his back.

It fell to the ground silently but he briefly turned at the slight *T* sound Bella's mouth had made, but she stood there, innocent to look at, dark in her thoughts, and he carried on walking.

Bella sat in the church for a suitable time, shaking at the enormity of what she was about to do, while sure that she had her mother's blessing, and then she gave her a kiss and left her.

Into her small house she went.

Bella knew Malvolio would still be watching her.

She would be seen on the train platform and if she hitchhiked… Bella thought of Matteo and his fear when that red car had pulled up alongside him.

There was only one way out.

Bella took her mother's silver hairbrush and one

of her heavy perfume bottles and, with the ring she had taken from her mother today, it was all she had.

She filled a bottle with some water and took some pastries that Sylvia had brought and then, after one last look around, Bella left her home, though tonight she went through the kitchen window.

Alongside the road out of Bordo Del Cielo ran the ocean but to the other side was the forest, and from long days and nights spent exploring while her mother had *entertained*, Bella knew the land well.

The dark did not scare her.

She embraced it because now it acted as her friend, hiding her as she ran through the night, the giant holly trees serving as her shield, and finally she made it to the ancient baths.

Bella stopped and had a drink and ate one of the pastries and took a moment to breathe and admire her beautiful surroundings.

It was her favourite place on earth and Bella looked up at the arches and columns and then down towards the deep stone baths, and she imagined them alive and beautiful again. She could only smile when she thought of the drunken, delicious debauchery that would have gone on there. 'You were born in the wrong time,' Bella said out loud to her mother, because she would have been revered back then. 'I'm sorry I won't be there to say goodbye…'

She said it here and then on through the night she went. The moon was sinking and the darkness would soon be gone but Bella knew where she was heading.

Finally she stepped out from the forest and there,

in the distance, she saw the lights of a gas station ahead and Bella knew that she was on the edge of the next town.

Her mother had told her about this place.

It was here her mother would come if she needed money that Malvolio didn't know about.

The sun was up by the time Bella walked in and she headed straight for the pay phone. Dialling Matteo's number, she fed in coins.

A woman answered.

'Can I speak with Matteo?'

'No,' came the breathless reply, 'because then he'd have to stop what he's doing.'

She could hear sounds in the background and it was painfully clear what was taking place as the woman ended the call.

Bella rang again but this time there was no answer, and as she put down the receiver her shoulders sagged and she just leant against the wall, not knowing what to do.

'Mi dica?'

A man asked if there was anything that Bella wanted.

'I'm trying to get to Rome.'

'I'm going as far as Messina…' he offered.

'Now?' Bella checked.

'Now.'

They headed out to his huge truck and Bella climbed in and turned to thank him but then she saw that he had opened his zipper.

'First, though…' he said, and Bella turned to get out, to run back into the shop, but then, in the side-view mirror, Bella saw a red car pulling up.

It was after seven.

She had been running all through the night, only for Malvolio to catch her here.

'Drive,' Bella said. 'We can pull over a little further up.'

'In a hurry?' he checked, and Bella nodded. She could see Malvolio striding into the shop and she turned and gave the driver a smile.

'Go, now,' Bella said. 'If you do I'll make it up to you soon.'

And she did.

To her eternal shame she did.

What had happened between her and Matteo had never in the least shamed her but now she understood what her mother had meant about stigma. Bella would never tell another person about this, not even Sophie, but from that morning on and to this very day Bella considered herself a whore.

CHAPTER ELEVEN

'*SALUTE*,' SAID SOPHIE, despite the early hour, and they chinked champagne glasses as the plane carried them home.

Luka was sitting, going through his phone, Paulo was being shown to the bedroom, and soon Bella would move behind a curtained area and carry on with the final details that would complete Sophie's dress.

'Are you okay, Bella?' Sophie asked. She could see, despite her smile, her friend's swollen eyes and she knew she had been crying.

'I will be.'

'Luka just told me that Matteo isn't bringing Shandy,' Sophie said. 'If that helps.'

'It makes no difference to me.' Bella shrugged and lied a little. 'I'm not upset about him. I feel bad because I always swore that when I came home it would be to give my mother a decent stone for her grave.'

She knew that Malvolio had seen that her mother had got a pauper's funeral.

'I have a little saved but I don't think it's going to be enough.'

'I feel terrible for using your savings...'

They had spent nearly all they had between them

so that Sophie could walk into Luka's office feeling proud but there was no need for Sophie to feel guilty and Bella shook her head. 'Please don't,' she said. 'We were always going to bring your father home.' They had thought it would be for his burial. 'At least we get to do it together, with champagne and with Paulo still alive. It has been money well spent.'

She smiled again but Sophie still didn't believe that was all.

'Bella, why do you still let Matteo think you're…?' Sophie glanced over and saw that Luka was still reading from his phone, but Bella knew what she was referring to and so answered without Sophie needing to elaborate.

'Because I don't want him to ever know how I really feel about him.'

'But why?'

'There's no point.' Bella shrugged.

'Because of Shandy?'

Because of me, Bella wanted to say, but held in her words.

She knew Sophie didn't get it—after all, she had no idea what had gone on during that trip from Sicily to Rome.

It was easier to act hardened in front of Matteo, to taunt and to tease than to reveal to him her truth—that she utterly loved him but, by his rules and her shame, Bella knew they could never be.

'Hey!' Bella, ever the chameleon, really did smile this time. 'Maybe he isn't bringing Shandy for a reason—even if we can't have a relationship, perhaps I might make enough money for my mother's stone!'

'Bella!' Sophie gave a shocked grin.

'Why not?' Bella sat there and laughed and actually warmed to the idea.

She hoped Luka didn't jilt her friend, not just to save Sophie the shame but also because the best man and bridesmaid would dance and she wanted just a few moments with him, to be held in his arms again before she somehow got on with the rest of her life. 'One night, no strings…' she said, but then she shook her head.

She couldn't do it to herself.

And, anyway, those hours spent last night crying bitterly about the past had served her well.

She wanted a better future.

'After the wedding, and after I have given my mother a decent headstone, I am going to save up again…'

'For?'

'For me,' Bella said. 'I am going to apply one last time to design school and if that fails then I am going to have business cards made up and start a proper business. I'm going to make something of myself,' Bella said. 'I'm going to make the Gatti name something every woman wants to have in her wardrobe…' She laughed as she stood. 'Rather than what every man wants in the bedroom.'

She left Sophie laughing and moved to another seat and got on with stitching the tiny buttons onto Sophie's dress. Last night's reminiscing had put her behind but it was still all coming together beautifully.

When they got to Bordo Del Cielo she would remove the tissue paper and add a few final touches, then it would be gently hand-washed.

Bella had no modesty where her dressmaking was concerned, she knew it was going to be beautiful.

Sophie might just be about to become Sicily's most beautiful jilted bride!

Bordo Del Cielo brimmed with memories—some painful and some so beautiful that they brought a different kind of agony. As they drove along the street that would take them to Paulo's home, there was the welling of tears in Bella's eyes and love in her heart for the land she missed every day.

At every turn of her head Bella wanted to let out a cry of recognition.

There was the river, where Matteo had got to on the night he had tried to escape.

A little further and there was a small lookout, where tourists stopped to take in the valley of forest, often missing the shaded path that would take them down to the baths.

On they drove and as the hotel came into view Bella remembered not the hours she had worked there or her fear in the bar but a night being made love to by Matteo.

Only from the beach would she be able to see the window of their room but as they turned off the main road Bella craned her neck for another glimpse, because, for her, true love had been found there.

Even the air tasted better, Bella thought as they stepped out of the car and took the path to Paulo's old house.

'We'll go to the beach, to our secret cove...' Bella said, as excited as a child on their holidays, but for now Sophie had to sort out her father, for the journey, albeit luxurious, had depleted him.

Luka declined coffee and said that he was heading to the hotel and Bella's ears pricked up when he said that he was meeting with Matteo.

He must be here.

She showered and changed into a short black skirt and a pretty top that she pinched from Sophie then added earrings and did her make-up with care.

'You look lovely.' Sophie smiled.

'Thank you, but it isn't for Matteo.'

She would walk the streets of home with pride.

'I might go for a walk,' Bella said. 'I would like to look at my old home, even if there are others living there.'

She soon found her home and it looked as if it was vacant. The flowerbeds that her mother had so carefully attended to were full of weeds and the windows were dusty and she had to wipe them to peer in.

Bella frowned because, though the furnishings seemed covered in sheets, it looked as if little had been moved or changed. It made no sense because Bella knew that property prices had soared since Malvolio's death. Bordo Del Cielo was a tourist destination yet her old home seemed untouched.

She had left the place in haste. She hadn't even spent a full night there since her mother's collapse and she knew what she wanted to do.

She headed back to Paulo's and there was a note from Sophie saying she had gone to the cemetery and Bella had the house to herself for a little while. She took the tissue paper out of the dress and used Rosa's ancient sewing machine to sew two last blind seams and then, hearing them come back, Bella bundled the dress into a bag.

'Are you going for another walk?' Sophie smiled when she again headed out.

'Who knows who I might bang into.' Bella smiled because she was a tease, even with her friends.

She always did her best to keep things light, even if her heart was heavy.

Yet it wasn't heavy today.

It was starting to heal.

Bella managed the kitchen window easily and was soon climbing in and she was home.

Finally home.

She remembered the terror of leaving, and that terror left her a little today.

She took off all the dust sheets and washed the windows so that sun streamed in, and she scrubbed down the floors because her mother had always been proud.

She went into her wardrobe and took out a dress of ginger and set to work with scissors and thread and then washed and hung it.

Then Bella washed Sophie's gown with much loving care and, having rolled it in a towel and gently squeezed out the excess water, she hung it outside to dry in the Sicilian sun as she tended the little garden.

Bella pulled out weeds and exposed flowers that her mother had always loved.

She picked a bunch. Some had been planted, others were wild, and Maria would have adored each and every one.

She walked up the hill and into the churchyard.

Five years late for her own mother's funeral, Bella

knelt at her grave and what she saw brought happy tears to her eyes.

Yes, she had been given a pauper's grave but there was a wooden cross and her name had been written on it and there were flowers, some new, some fading.

Yes, she had been loved by many.

No, she had not been forgotten.

CHAPTER TWELVE

THE WEDDING DAY dawned and Matteo walked with Luka along the shore.

They were still in the suits they had worn last night.

They had drunk far too much, reminisced too much, and now as they walked to clear their heads, a vision clouded Matteo's.

There was Bella. She was in a loose dress, her hair was down and blowing in the wind, and she was a dangerous sight for sore eyes.

'Bella.' Luka nodded to her.

'If you are going to marry my friend I hope you meet with a razor, and if you're to be the best man,' she added to Matteo, 'then I suggest the same.'

'How is Sophie this morning?' Luka asked, as Matteo stood silent beside him.

'She's fine,' Bella said. 'And she'll be fine, whatever happens today. I doubt you can say the same.'

'Meaning?'

'I love my friend,' Bella said. 'I can't imagine my world without her. You can tell me what that world is like tomorrow perhaps…'

She went to walk off.

'Is Sophie at home?' Luka asked.

'She's at the cove,' Bella said, not turning her head. She was furious with Luka and what he was about to do.

She didn't turn around, even when she heard footsteps coming up behind her and her name being called, but Matteo caught her wrist and he swung her around to face him.

And it wasn't disgust she had seen in his eyes that day by the Trevi Fountain, Bella realised, it had been anger, and he was unleashing some of it now.

'I gave you an out!' he shouted. 'I understand that your mother was ill but I left you enough money to leave later...'

Bella let out a hollow laugh, shrugged off his hand and kept on walking.

'Gina took her share, Malvolio his, and what was left...' She shrugged. 'Three months of meals at the hospital, toiletries, and I bought my mother a scarf and some bed slippers and things. Do you want me to make a list?' She turned and looked at Matteo.

'You only needed to call, Bella.'

'You didn't give me your number.'

'You could have called Luka.'

'Have you forgotten just how poor Malvolio kept us?' Bella raged. 'I could have looked up his name on my laptop maybe, or used up the credit on my cellphone, trying to find him. Oh, but that's right, I don't have either. I had call boxes and coins, and when I got home my phone had been cut off. But I *did* call you, Matteo. My mother died the day after Paulo was sentenced...' She watched as his face paled a little and he started to piece together the dates. 'I got your number and I ran through a forest to escape and I did call

you, but you were otherwise engaged.' She looked
him square in the eye and, no, she did not need dark
glasses to hide behind any more. 'Did you love her?'

'Who?'

'The woman you were busy with through that
night…'

He had been trying to bleach out the thought of
Bella and Dino. 'Bella,' Matteo admitted, 'I can't even
remember who she was…'

'Exactly,' she said. 'I know this much about her,
though, and all the other women since. They loved
your money. So tell me, who's the real whore?'

Matteo didn't answer.

'Did you ever think to call me?' she asked.

'I called over and over,' Matteo said, 'and when
you didn't answer, I called Dino…'

They both knew what he had said.

Matteo cleared his throat. 'Luka has gone to talk
to Sophie,' he said, about to suggest that they do the
same, but Bella was too angry to let him finish.

'I don't need your running commentary, Matteo,'
she said. 'I'll hear what's happening from my friend.
How is the hotel?' She glanced up at it and from here
she could see the room they had shared that night and
bitterness rose in her chest. 'It's just as well Shandy
isn't here, it would be a let-down after Fiscella.'

'Not to me,' he said, for he had one very pleasant
memory of that place.

She looked back at him.

'I'm in the same room,' he said. 'It hasn't changed
a bit.'

'Oh, so what time do you want me there?'

'Bella!' he shouted at her. 'I didn't say it for that. I

meant that I'm in the same room…' And he screwed his eyes closed because how did you flirt with a whore? How did you tell her that the memories were killing him and it was agony to be back here?

A beautiful, black agony because it had kept him in the bar all night rather than go back to the room without her there.

'Do you want me in a maid outfit?' Bella said. 'While your fiancée is away, we can play, perhaps…'

'Yes…'

He would have her again, he would empty his wallet for her again, he would do anything he could just to go back to that night.

There was no thought really, just that.

His kiss was rough, it was fierce, she had been goading him, shaming herself, sure, just sure he would tell her where to get off, that Matteo Santini would not want her in the same way that he once had.

Yet he did.

It hurt. There were tears of shock as she kissed him back. It hurt her soul to taste again what she craved, and now, to give in, she was back at day one, aching with withdrawal, and so even as their tongues thrashed, even as their groins displayed their devotion, somehow, somehow she pushed him back. And then she said not that he couldn't afford her but the truth.

'I can't afford to.'

For if she did, surely she lost her soul?

Matteo returned to that room and he lay on the bed, staring at the ceiling fan, rather glad of the seedy surroundings.

It had seemed luxurious at the time.

The memory still was.

He had spent five years fulfilling his promise to himself. He had let go of the past, built a reputation, and while he would throw it all away this very moment, still he thought of the impact on her.

Either face the press or live in isolation...

He thought of the sheikh he was meeting with soon to discuss a chain of hotels and how hard it would be on Bella to introduce her as his wife after the salacious headlines had hit...

Matteo was lying there, thinking of throwing everything he had worked for away for Bella, and he knew that he needed out of this place.

A clear head was not possible with her around.

'Hey.' Matteo was still lying on the bed in a prison cell called Bella when the reluctant groom called.

'The wedding's happening,' Luka said. 'For real. I don't need a lecture. Sophie and I—'

'I don't need to hear it.'

He didn't want to know his friend had found love, he didn't want to know that he must now dance with Bella tonight.

He wanted his helicopter and he wanted it now. He wanted to be lifted out of the sky and back to the safe haven he had created, where women came loudly and then left, hopefully, quietly.

Instead, a few hours later he stood in a packed church.

All the locals were there.

Past sins forgiven.

But it was not the bride he noticed as Sophie walked down the aisle but the bridesmaid.

Bella was wearing a dress and the colour was ginger and Matteo knew it was the one she had worn for the Natalia party the night he hadn't shown up.

It was.

She had made a few modifications.

The back was lower and the sleeves were gone.

It showed her slender figure, it brought out the deepest green of her eyes.

Yes, she knew how to dress as a lady and today she was one.

She gave him a very soft smile and then she focussed on the wedding and tried not to cry, because while she would love her friend for ever and did not begrudge her a moment of this day, there was a special pain, a unique loneliness that came when your friend found love.

Bella suddenly felt left behind.

Alone.

With her pride, though, Bella reminded herself.

It was a beautiful wedding but it wasn't theirs.

Bella and Matteo walked out with the happy couple onto the street and there were cheers and celebration rice was being thrown.

There were drinks to be drunk and speeches to be made, and they did it all and looked out to the street with the olive trees dressed in lights that started to sparkle as evening came. There was no choice but to hold each other again as they danced that one dance.

It was cruel.

It was bliss.

She sank into his arms and he wrapped them around her just because.

He felt the same, Bella thought, he smelt the same, only *she* wasn't the same.

'I'm sorry that I offended you this morning,' he said, and she looked up to him and nodded. 'You offended your fiancée too,' Bella said. 'I don't like her but don't be that man who cheats.' She said the same words she had on the night they had found each other. 'I thought better of you.'

He was better than that, and it mattered enough to tell her.

'We broke up,' he said, 'about ten minutes after you got fired.'

'I don't believe you,' Bella said. 'You say that just so I agree to go back to your room with you.'

'No,' he said. 'I'm saying that because this morning wasn't about cheating or lying, it was about us and my wanting you.'

'You didn't think to tell me?'

'Oh, I did,' he said, and she frowned as he spoke on. 'I decided it was safer not to.'

'Were you worried that you might have called down for room service?' Bella smiled just a little and so too did he.

'Yep.'

Then he broke the last piece of her heart.

'I'm leaving after this dance,' he said, and from the strain in his voice she knew that he meant it. 'I've booked a helicopter—'

'You're the best man.'

'I know,' he said, 'but I have to go and I have to think and I can't do that with you…'

He couldn't, because he was as turned on as she was. If he stayed, if there was even one more dance they would be back in the hotel room and tonight Matteo needed to be the best man he could be.

Not for Luka but for Bella and himself.

He kissed her cheek and said goodbye and he held her a moment and smelt her hair and then she watched as he went and said farewell to the bride and groom. She saw the lights of his helicopter and Bella stood alone.

With her pride, though.

It offered little consolation.

CHAPTER THIRTEEN

BELLA WASN'T A MAGPIE.

She didn't take shiny things for herself.

The nice things she wanted were for the people she loved.

Tonight, though, her desire was selfish.

'Sophie…' Bella went over to her friend and Sophie was the happiest she had ever seen her. It was clear to all that this wedding was no farce—you could feel the love between Sophie and Luka.

'I'm going to be the worst bridesmaid in the world,' Bella said, and Sophie smiled as she told her that she would be leaving early.

'Are you going after the best man?'

Bella nodded. 'I'll never be suitable wife material for Matteo,' she said, 'I get that, but…' She didn't finish. She didn't need to explain to her friend that the one night she'd had with Matteo was one she had fought for five years not to remember.

Bella wanted one more night that she would never let herself forget.

'Go,' Sophie said, and they had a cuddle. 'Do you need a car?'

'No, I've asked Pino to take me.'

Bella slipped away from the wedding party and into the churchyard and past the beautiful gravestones, then she went back to her mother's grave, which the villagers still dressed with kindness.

'I love you, Ma. I love you so much and one day I'll be back to give you the stone you deserve, but tonight I'm leaving. I'm going to spend the money I've saved on myself. I'm going to do something not because I have to but because I want to.'

Pino, the village messenger, had moved from a bicycle to a moped and now lived a very clean life, but at Bella's insistence he rode faster.

Yes, it was freeing to take the road out of Bordo Del Cielo that would lead her to Matteo.

They drove alongside the ocean with the forest that had saved her on the other side and finally she was free to make her own choices, however unwise they might be.

She took the last flight out and was back at her flat by the small hours, and as she showered only then did Bella remember that she was supposed to be back at work at six to start the breakfasts.

With all that had happened in recent days, she had forgotten to swap her shift.

She wore no make-up as she pulled on a green uniform and her sensible lace-up shoes. She might regret it tomorrow but right now she would follow her heart.

And Matteo followed his.

He arrived in Rome to a packed city that felt empty, and after a short time away from Bella his head was already completely clear.

The decision he had been coming to since he had stood, right here at this fountain, was made now, and he took the coin from his pocket and tossed it in.

He would be back and with her by his side.

And if that were the case, there was a lot he needed to do.

He arrived back at the hotel and made the necessary phone calls and then he fell into a dreamless sleep.

Or, rather, it was dreamless at first.

CHAPTER FOURTEEN

BELLA HAD NEVER been scared of the dark and she wasn't now.

She walked down the alley at the side of the hotel and went in through the workers' entrance, but she did not head to the kitchens where her shift was due to start later.

Instead, she took an elevator up to the top floors where she didn't usually work.

She took out her swipe card and told herself that if he was not alone, there would be no more water-throwing, she would simply turn and leave.

She lied to herself!

But he *was* alone.

She knew it the second she walked in and saw him lying there. Matteo was asleep on his back and she stood a moment, allowing her eyes to adjust. He was far less careful with his clothes than yesteryear because they were all tossed on the floor, along with a couple of towels. She moved her gaze and took in the delicious sight of him. One arm was up over his head, his other hand was on his flat stomach and the sheet just covered him.

Bella walked over quietly and she wanted to wake

him with a kiss but her fingers were too impatient to await instruction. Already they were on his shoulder and, feeling his skin beneath her fingers, she ran her hand down his arm, feeling him, as if testing that he was real.

Matteo fought not to wake. In his dream she was standing there, her fragrance, her touch, the perfection his senses knew.

He let out a breath and his hand moved a little lower on his stomach but then it was halted by hers and Bella lowered her head and kissed her sleeping beauty.

It was a soft kiss but sinful with seduction. As his lips parted her tongue slipped in and she hovered over him, holding his wrist, loving his mouth and the fact that he didn't open his eyes.

It was a kiss that had her move over him and the feel of his hands on her hips, guiding her, was sublime. Still he did not open his eyes.

'Am I dreaming?' Matteo said, between slow kisses.

'Maybe we both are.'

His hand dealt with the bow of her apron and then he undid the poppers on her robe and reacquainted himself with her naked breasts. She terminated their kiss and sat on his thighs, taking his lovely erection. It was, for Bella, healing to hold Matteo in her palm over and over.

'How do you want me?' she said.

'Exactly as you are.'

She didn't understand his meaning, it just felt like a very nice thing to hear as he pulled her up and lifted the skirt of her dress.

His eyes were now open, watching her lower herself onto him, and Bella let out a sob of remembrance and bliss as finally he was back to being her lover.

Matteo tore at her dress to remove it. He wanted to watch their reunion; he wanted to revisit every inch of naked skin.

'Careful,' Bella warned. 'I have to do the breakfasts at six…'

He shredded her dress despite the warning.

That she would fly through the night to give him this morning without knowing of his plans for them, that she would embrace one last depravity with him had Matteo pull her down to his mouth to kiss fiercely the only love he had known in his life.

He rolled her, yet they rolled in unison and she knotted her ankles as he moved to his elbows.

Their mouths were brutal, their bodies each other's to own again, and right now Bella did not care for how long.

'You left the wedding to come here?'

Bella nodded. 'I knew as soon as you'd gone that I'd made a mistake. I have never regretted our times together, it's the times we're apart that are filled with remorse. I know that we can't go anywhere.'

'You don't know that.'

'But I do. I remember you saying, once a killer always a killer, once a whore—'

'Bella,' Matteo interrupted her, 'I said that when I lived in Malvolio's black and white world. Those were words we were raised on but we are away from all that now.'

'True words, though,' Bella said, and she told him a little of what had happened with her mother and her father. 'He looked at her with disgust when he found out what she had done.'

'Have I ever looked at you in disgust?' Matteo asked.

'No, but you don't know what I did.'

'Did?' Matteo checked.

'When I was trying to get to Rome.'

'Tell me.'

'I can't.'

'I think you have to, Bella,' he said, not because he needed salacious detail, but because he didn't understand. She had taunted him, flirted with him, come to him intending to pop out and serve breakfast afterwards! He was starting to realise that this side of Bella was exclusive to him and he could feel her shame, her pain for whatever it was that had gone on. 'Bella, you can tell me anything.'

She looked up at him and realised that she could.

It had not been disgust she had seen in his eyes, it had been anger, and that had all gone now.

'I've never told anybody.'

'Then change that now.'

Bella nodded because her secret felt as if it was choking her.

So she told him about that night, how she had tried to get to the phone but Malvolio had been watching. And she told him how she had run through the forest and stopped by the ancient baths.

'Then I saw the gas station and I was starting to think I had made it. I called you but I could not get through to you. A man offered me a lift to Messina. He was older and I honestly thought that he was being kind, then we got into the cabin and he…' She cringed at the memory.

'Did he force you?'

'No.' That was the part Bella was most ashamed about. 'I went to leave but then I saw Malvolio's car pull up…'

Matteo knew, better than anyone, the fear that would have induced.

'I could see Malvolio,' she said, her eyes filling with tears. 'If he had seen me I would have been taken back or maybe worse. And so I told the man, not here, I gave him a smile and I said we would stop further along the road. He knew I was in a hurry to get away and so we drove for a short distance and then…'

'And then?'

He had thought there had been many, but that it had been just one made it worse in some ways, for she hadn't become deadened and her eyes were not vacant, and he could feel how much it must have distressed her.

'And then,' Bella said, and she lifted her hand and made a lewd gesture, and Matteo looked at her and didn't blink. He just thought about her lonely on the edge of the woods, unsafe and scared, and he told her the very truth.

'*I'd* have given him a hand job, Bella.' She tried to smile at his joke but then realised that he was completely serious. 'If I had been in that situation, I would have given the bastard whatever he wanted just to get away. I'm sorry you had to do it but I'm very proud of you that you did.'

Never, in all the stinging, agonising scenarios that

she'd taunted herself with, had Bella imagined the word 'proud' being there in Matteo's response.

'I'm so proud of you, Bella, for getting out.'

'Thank you.' She gave him a little smile but it was a real one.

'And after Messina?'

'I got another ride and this time it was all the way through to Rome,' Bella said. 'I was terrified but the man was nice. He gave me some of his soup and he chatted about his family. But that other one…' She shuddered. 'It was the worst two minutes of my life.'

'Two minutes!'

'My mother had taught me a few tricks of the trade and had told me the words to say when you just wanted it over and done.'

'And they were?'

She was one burning blush, and he could feel the scorch of her cheeks as her mouth came to his ear.

And so she told him her very choice words and she waited for anger, for his appalled response.

'That'd do it, Bella,' he said, and to her shock he started to laugh.

'It was awful…' she said.

'I know, but you got it over and done with and you're here.' Then he picked up her hand and kissed it slowly and made it beautiful again.

Oh, he was lovely, he took her in his arms, he held her and he told her all the terrible things he had done, all the seamier stuff and the terrible stuff, and now he told her about his scar and how he'd deserved that knife. And then he told her the memory that still taunted him, walking into the bedroom from the shower that morning and seeing the bruise on her face that his hand had made.

Bella looked at him, and she loathed how she had taunted him with it the other day.

'You saved me from hell that night,' she said, and she picked up his hand and kissed away the shame as he had done to her, but there was a knock at the door and Bella gave a little yelp when she saw the time.

'I have to do breakfast…' She went to get out of bed but he halted her and then the knock came again.

'Breakfast is here,' Matteo said. 'Let's hope for a less clumsy maid this time.'

'I have to hide…'

'Stay there,' he said. 'You don't ever have to hide again.'

She sat there, covered by the sheet, as Alfeo came in.

To his credit he hesitated for just the briefest moment when he saw Bella, before greeting his most esteemed guest. '*Buongiorno*, Signor Santini.' He glanced over at Bella. '*Signorina.*'

She had no words.

Perhaps used to Matteo's ways and assuming he might have a guest, just not that particular one, Alfeo had two cups and he offered to pour the coffee.

Matteo nodded.

As Alfeo served the coffee he told Matteo that his helicopter would be ready in half an hour, as he had requested, and then, to Bella's relief, he left.

'There goes my job!'

'You're in bed with the boss, though.' Matteo smiled but Bella didn't return it.

'You have to go soon.'

'Actually, I don't,' he said. 'Bella, helicopters don't fly to Dubai, I've postponed that trip. The helicopter is to take me to Bordo Del Cielo.'

'Why would you go there?'

'Because that is where I thought you would be this morning,' he said. 'By the time I landed in Rome I knew the mistake I had made and we have made so many mistakes, Bella, and though many were not of our making, this one was mine. I wanted to tell you I loved you yesterday but I waited a day too long. I wanted it sorted this morning.' He leant over her and on the bedside table was a small, highly polished box that, Bella knew, came from the very exclusive jewellers in the hotel. 'I had them wake up the jeweller last night,' Matteo said. 'I was coming to Bordo Del Cielo this morning to ask you to be my wife.'

'What if the press find out about me?'

'It wasn't a very illustrious career, Bella. There's one sad old man and if he comes forward he'll have me to deal with. You might have heard—I'm not always this nice.' Then he looked right into her eyes. 'And I don't count because we loved each other, even then.'

'What about my mother?'

'You're proud of her?' Matteo checked, and Bella nodded.

'Then they can't touch you,' he said.

Bella lay in bed, admiring the ring on her finger, and Matteo called down to cancel the helicopter and for the tray to be removed. They settled in for a day in bed, but as he picked up the newspaper something caught his eye and he recalled Bella's words.

'It would take just one beautiful woman to make the headlines wearing one of my gowns.'

Matteo unfolded the paper and there was Sophie and Luka on their wedding day. Somehow, despite it being a local affair, their photo had already made it to the press. It was news indeed that Malvolio's son had married the daughter of his right-hand man…but Matteo skimmed past all that, it was history, it was past. He was more interested in the future so he read out loud to Bella the more pertinent part.

'"The bride wore a white chiffon gown by Gatti—an emerging designer who is based in Rome".' He turned and smiled as Bella just about fell off the bed.

'You've made it, Bella.'

On her own she had made it, she realised, but now she shared the future with him.

EPILOGUE

BELLA STOOD IN the home that she had once lived in with her mother.

It was hers now.

Sophie had been the one to tell her that Luka was doing all he could to reverse some of the damage that his father had done and that the deeds had been signed over to Bella.

It had remained untouched, in the same way Paulo's had, because Malvolio's plan had been to tear down more buildings and build yet another hotel.

Instead, the pretty town remained.

Today the house was dressed with flowers from the garden and so too was the bride.

Flowers that her mother had planted dotted Bella's hair and were in the tied bouquet she would carry.

'Your dress is amazing,' Sophie said. 'Though I think shoe designers everywhere are going to hate you very soon.'

The bride wore Gatti!

It was the most delicate Sicilian lace with a scoop neckline and it fell loose on her slender figure and, given the intricate fabric, Bella had decided it needed no more.

No make-up, no perfume, no curls and no shoes, just a dress spun in the lace of home, flowers from her mother's garden and Bella's smile.

Late afternoon they stopped at the church and left flowers on her mother's beautiful stone, one that Bella had had laid in a moving service.

The villagers still left flowers and she smiled when she remembered her mother telling her she'd had her share of lovers.

Roses amongst the thorns.

'I'm happy, Ma,' Bella said. 'Matteo is the most wonderful man. Soon we will start our new life in London...'

And Rome.

Or perhaps Dubai.

The demand for Bella's work was starting to grow, both here and overseas. With Matteo's impressive property portfolio, where they were based wasn't an issue.

'I'm not scared of the press any more,' Bella said, though her words were braver than she perhaps felt. There had been an article in a rather plummy paper alluding to Bella Gatti's impoverished past and that she had been the only child of a single mother.

The article had left a slight unease in Bella's stomach but she remembered Matteo's words.

She was proud of her mother.

She took some flowers from her bouquet and placed them on the stone then she returned to the car and they drove on along the one road out of Bordo Del Cielo till they came to the small lookout. That was where the car stopped and Sophie and Bella got out.

Behind the lookout there was a path that could easily be missed and down the trail they went. The moss was cool beneath Bella's bare feet. All the trees were dotted with lights to lead the way and then like an oasis there they were—at the ancient baths that Bella loved so.

There too the trees and columns were lit with tiny lights, and the stone tables were piled high with the awaiting feast. Everyone in the village had made the same journey down the path and they were waiting for the bride to arrive. The ancient baths were alive again.

Luka was the best man and stood beside Matteo. Matteo looked more handsome than ever and was wearing a dark suit and a tie that was the same mossy green as her eyes. There was no one to give her away but there was no need for a substitute, she went alone, willing to be by his side.

'Babe in the woods,' Matteo said when she joined him. 'You look as if you just stepped into my dream.'

He was always in hers.

As they said their vows, just before he went to place the ring on her finger Matteo lifted her hand and kissed her palm deeply.

Only they knew what that meant and Bella did the same to him.

They forgave their pasts as together they embraced the future. So much had been against them and yet love had won.

It was a stunning party in the most incredible location and to dance with Matteo under the moonlight and to know they were finally together made Bella sure she was the luckiest person alive, and she told him so.

'Second luckiest,' he said.

When it was time for the happy couple to leave, Bella embraced her friend.

'It's time to be happy, Bella,' Sophie said, and Bella nodded.

'For you too,' she said.

In a couple of days' time they would again sit together at their secret cove and catch up properly, just as they had done while growing up.

Tonight, though, was for Matteo and Bella.

No one could quite understand why, with helicopters and planes at his disposal, Matteo would insist that their wedding night be spent at Brezza Oceana. And certainly the staff there could not fathom why Matteo Santini had not asked for the best room but also for a bottle of the cheapest wine.

Oh, and nuts.

This time, when Bella stepped into the room she was happy and laughing.

Matteo opened the windows and put on the music they had danced to all that time ago.

'I've got a present for you,' she said, and she went into the bag she had left in the room and she watched as he opened it and took out the pregnancy test card. 'I forgot one thing when I came to your room that night.'

Matteo stared at it for a very long time and then he looked at Bella.

'Well, I'm very glad that you did.'

'Surprised?'

'No,' he said. 'Happy. I never thought I'd have a family…' And now he had a wife and also the news that he would be a father. 'Barefoot and pregnant,' Matteo said, and then he looked down at her feet. 'You need a bath.'

'I do.'

'I'll go and get it ready while you open your present.'

Bella looked at the thin package that was on the bed and as Matteo left to run the water, she peeled open the silver paper and then opened an envelope and took a moment to read it.

She sat on the bed for ages, just looking out at the view and wondering how she could be so lucky, so happy, so deeply in love and, best of all, so very loved.

When Matteo called to her she went through to the bathroom and saw that he was already in.

'You've bought this hotel?'

'*We've* bought this hotel,' Matteo said. 'Just us. This isn't a part of the business Luka and I have.' He explained his thinking. 'The happiest time of my life, before you, was here. I love the place and I love being here again. I could see that with better management and a massive refurbishment we could turn this place into a jewel. The people will be happy because there will be fewer tourists, albeit richer ones, and…' He looked at Bella, who just stood at the door. 'When I thought your past might be a touch more colourful I tried to think of a place where the people would look out for you,' he said. 'There are no secrets now, and so I knew nothing that might be revealed would be news to them. The people of Bordo Del Cielo will also take care of you.'

That he would take such tender care of her heart brought tears to Bella's eyes.

'Our baby will be born here,' she said.

'And grow up here. Though there will be a lot of

travel with my work and yours, I thought that it might be nice to have here as our base.'

It was more than nice, Bella thought. He had brought her home.

This time it was Matteo who lay in the bath as she undressed.

The dress was loose enough that she could lift it easily over the head and he watched as she hung it on the hook.

She took off her bra and slid down her panties and Matteo smiled. No shoes, no stockings, no garters, she stood naked and wearing only a smile.

'Grooms everywhere are going to appreciate your work, Bella.'

'You have to think about taking the dress off, I will tell my brides. Not just putting it on.'

She climbed in and was trembling with the enormity of it all as she joined him.

To be here with Matteo, as his wife, meant that it was the perfect wedding night for Bella, and she told him so as they kissed.

Memories wrapped around them like the steam from the bath. Sensual memories of times before and all that was to come.

She wrapped her legs around him and Matteo held her steady as they looked deep into each other's eyes and he took her for the first time as his wife.

It was the gentlest coupling, the deepest and most intense feeling as now they could both look and touch.

Yes, they remembered the longing as they had lain on that grassy knoll, a safe distance from each other, and made love with their eyes.

Then he smiled at her temper and the ice-cold water

that had doused him that morning in Hotel Fiscella and he pulled her down a little harder.

Her shoulders were tense and her neck felt as if it needed to stretch, but that would mean she left the gaze of his eyes.

'I love you for ever,' he said, and she toppled forward, resting her head on his shoulder as she started to come.

The water barely moved, there was just the lap at the edges as he came deep inside. There was little to denote all that took place beneath the calm surface but they knew the deep pleasure the other gave. Matteo moved her head back so that he could see her.

'Come to bed,' he said. 'Come to bed with me to-night and be my lover for the rest of my life.'

As he had all those years ago, he carried her there. This time the French windows were open. Now there was just the sound of the ocean and a lot of love to be made.

It was a view to live for.

* * * * *

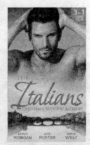

MILLS & BOON®

It's Got to be Perfect

IT'S GOT
TO BE
Perfect

UNCORRECTED
PROOF COPY

HALEY HILL

* cover in development

When Ellie Rigby throws her three-carat engagement ring into the gutter, she is certain of only one thing. She has yet to know true love!

Fed up with disastrous internet dates and conflicting advice from her friends, Ellie decides to take matters into her own hands. Starting a dating agency, Ellie becomes an expert in love. Well, that is until a match with one of her clients, charming, infuriating Nick, has her questioning everything she's ever thought about love…

Order yours today at
www.millsandboon.co.uk